MY OWN WORST ENEMY

MY OWN WORST ENEMY

Carol Sonenklar

AN
APPLE
PAPERBACK

SCHOLASTIC INC.

New York Toronto London Auckland Sydney
Mexico City New Delhi Hong Kong

To my parents,
Sol and Hilda Sonenklar
C. S.

ACKNOWLEDGMENT

A special thanks to Pat Yost
and her seventh grade English class
at Mount Nittany Middle School
C. S.

ISBN 0-439-17518-6

12 11 10 9 8 7 6 5 4 3   0 1 2 3 4 5/0

Printed in the U.S.A.   40

First Scholastic printing, September 2000

CHAPTER ONE

I was standing in front of my mirror, doing a brilliant impersonation of my brother's girlfriend, Alicia, when the topic first came up. Imagining a baby tee and chunky platforms instead of my bleach-stained U of M sweatshirt and holey red Keds, I'd finally gotten it perfectly: the tilt of her chin, the mock-angry little pout, the arms folded up high on the chest, and most important, the baby voice ("A-wee-shuh angwee at Daavvee-y"). How was I supposed to know that my father was watching me from the hallway?

And now we were sitting on my bed having another "little chat." The imitation had been for the benefit of my chocolate Labrador, Rita. She and she alone appreciated my comedic gifts. She'd wag her tail when I talked to her in "A-wee-shuh speak." ("Sit, Wee-tah!") But my dad didn't look amused, and that's when he asked the fateful question:

"Why don't you take this opportunity to turn over a new leaf?"

Sure, the question sounded harmless, but I knew the deeper, more sinister implications; I'd already thought about it plenty. (It being that I wasn't too popular as the old leaf.) This brings me to the first of my many problems: I think too much. Now, don't get me wrong, here, I'm not some genius or something. No, I think too much about stuff that bugs me; I have the brain that never sleeps. Since I like to write, I record some of it in an old notebook. I figure that when I become a famous writer, the stuff that bugs me will become profound insights into the human condition instead of never-ending complaints, as my mother says.

Problem number two is that some of this stuff sometimes seeps out of my mouth. I call these "mouth droppings." Mouth droppings escape from my lips before my brain has processed what effect they may have on my listener. Here's an example: "Oh, you changed your hair. Is it supposed to look that way? No, I like the way your forehead sticks out. If you want to look like Herman Munster."

My dad cleared his throat. "So, Eve, how about that fresh start?"

A new leaf. A fresh start. Who makes up clichés, anyway? What's wrong with an old leaf? Why does a start have to be "fresh?" When something is fresh, don't people just love wrecking it? Like a perfect fresh peach that's just sitting there, waiting for someone to take a chomp out of it? Then maybe it's dropped on the floor and gets a mushy brown spot or sits around too long and grows some disgusting, furry blue fungus like we grew in Mrs. Silva's science class last year. So eventually all fresh things get mushy, fungus, or eaten. Just the word "fresh" was making me feel a little like barfing.

"Eve?"

That fresh stuff right here? *That's* the brain that never sleeps.

"Why does a start have to be fresh?" I asked.

"Well," Dad began heartily. (That meant I wasn't going to like the answer.) "Moving to a new place is a great opportunity to reinvent yourself. You had some trouble at your old school. Your teacher and a lot of kids in your class didn't always appreciate your sense of humor." He paused. "Or your candor."

Translate: Nobody thought I was funny and I have a big mouth.

"Alicia is a very sweet girl," Dad went on. "She was simply giving you suggestions on new ways to fix yourself up. Do you need to make fun of her?"

"I guess not," I replied. "With that hairdo, it's not necessary."

Yep, you guessed it: a mouth dropping. I turned away and stared out the window. What I really wanted to say was, Yes, I *do* need to make fun of her. Who asked Alicia for her stupid suggestions? *I* didn't. Who would suggest something if she didn't think you needed it? And my father thought I needed it. Just add him to the list of people who thought that if I looked more like a "normal" girl, I would act like one.

Except that I didn't want to look like a normal girl. Or act like one.

And that . . . is problem number three.

Things That Bug Me
#18: Clichés

Adults think that they've experienced every single thing that kids go through, so they don't really listen or pay attention when things happen to you. They just tell you some old, worn-out, boring saying that someone told them when they were kids like, "That's the way the cookie crumbles," or "You can't cry over spilled milk," or "Don't make a mountain out of a molehill." So when I have a zit on my chin the size of a moon crater on school picture day, I'm supposed to get comfort and consolation when Dad says to me, "Remember, honey, beauty's only skin deep." In other words, people will gaze at my picture and think, Wow, anyone with a zit like that must be very deep.

   Also, doesn't anyone wonder why or how we all somehow know clichés? It's like we're born with it. Or . . . we're brainwashed. Think about it: How hard would it be to turn the entire human population into mindless cliché-repeating zombies? Not very. Parents are not too far from this now. You could warn them except that they wouldn't listen to you because you're a kid.

   Go figure.

CHAPTER TWO

At this moment, brainwashing sounded like a dream vacation. Who wouldn't rather repeat in a monotone, "Yes, Kwayzar, your wish is my command," than have to think about what is constantly going through my brain: Starting eighth grade in the *middle* of the school year. Anyone knows that for teenagers this could be a traumatic experience. I could have recurring nightmares or invent multiple personalities named Cody and Madison. But does anyone care? Of course not.

And to top it all off, my mother won't even be here to help me get adjusted to my new school because she's got a new job, which is why we've moved to this new city. And Dad has a new job, too, which is "househusband." He doesn't think this is a real job, so he always holds up his fingers to make quotes around the word, which makes Mom mad, since that was her job until now and she says it's harder than most jobs you get paid for.

The car company that Dad worked for "downsized," which means shrank. They didn't need as many people to work there, so Dad was "laid off," which means not having your job anymore. I was surprised that Dad, who was a parts distribution manager, wasn't happy about it, since he came home from the office mad a lot, especially at his boss, who he called a "big dummy." But the car company must've liked big dummies working for them, because Dad's boss wasn't fired and Dad was madder than I'd ever seen him. I was kind of sad because ever since I was a little girl I'd always loved fooling around at Dad's office, where there was lots of neat stuff and nice Mrs. Butler, his secretary.

For almost a year, Dad looked for a new job. During that time, Mom wanted to go back to work, but Dad didn't want her to. He said that she belonged at home with David and me. Not long after that, though, he stopped looking for a job. He also stopped shaving and started watching daytime television. When I got home from school, I would find my dad still in his pajamas in front of the tube, eating Cherry Garcia out of the container. Even though I knew this wasn't good for my dad, I couldn't help watching TV with him. My favorite was the *Psychic Home Shopping Network*, where people read your mind and told you what you wanted to buy. My dad bought a Garden Weasel, a Lint-B-Gone, and some *Brady Bunch* Commemorative Plates. When Mom found out, she turned sort of a whitish green and said she needed to make a phone call.

The next thing I knew, we were moving to a new city and I had to start a new school. I didn't really want to move, but I knew that my dad wasn't supposed to be in his pajamas all day if he wasn't sick, so I kept my mouth shut. Dad wasn't happy that Mom was going back to work and they had some bad arguments late at night. I hated hearing them. Rita and I would huddle on the floor under my flannel comforter and wait to hear my so-called brother's car pull into the driveway. But we always fell asleep first.

David is seven years older than me. He is so-called because he's home so rarely that I was eight by the time I figured out he was a member of our family. He's just around to drop his dirty clothes on the bathroom floor, shower, get some clean clothes, and eat anything good in the refrigerator. David just started studying exercise science at the local university. He also managed to find a new girlfriend already. He has a girlfriend every minute of his life, I kid you not. Well, maybe not every minute; if he breaks up with one it takes him about ten minutes to find a new one. So he has a girlfriend every fifty minutes of his life, excuse me.

Anyways, now it was January and we were in our new house. And Dad was clean-shaven again, not watching the shows, supposedly learning the mysteries of running a house. He was still using the dumb quotes, which got my mom mad. She said that taking care of the house was a huge, never-ending, and unappreciated job. But some of that was her own fault, since she was a little nuts when it came to keeping the house clean. If you took out a carton of milk, put it on the counter, and then reached for a glass, the milk was gone when you went to pour it. I never said anything, but secretly I agreed with Dad that Mom was a cleanaholic and that she made too much of a big deal out of everything.

And Mom has gone back to her old job: selling drugs. (Relax.) She's a sales representative for a big drug company. Mom sells to pharmacies in her "territory," which means the area she is supposed to sell to. Her territory is big; it covers three states: Wisconsin, Indiana, and part of Michigan, where we now live. So Mom will be spending a lot of time on the road. This means that I will be spending a lot of time with my dad, which I haven't done too much because, until his layoff, he was a "workaholic" (lots of "aholics" in our household). But at least he's not as neat or picky as Mom and doesn't like vegetables, either. He also probably won't care if I read this funny magazine I discovered called *DUH!*

The first time I saw *DUH!* was at my older cousin's house. The magazine has funny versions of television shows and movies and lots of cartoons about school and parents and stuff like that. I was laughing so hard that my mom got curious and looked through it. She thought the humor was "a bit sophisticated" and wouldn't let me get a subscription. So I sneak it into the house when I can.

Here's the reason I love *DUH!:* When I opened it, I discovered a place filled with people who were bugged by the same things I was bugged by—stuff that was unfair or made no sense or set rules for some people but not for others.

I'd always figured there was nothing you could do about stuff like that. But when I found *DUH!*, I saw that there was something you could do about it: You could make fun of it, thumb your nose at it, stick your tongue out at it. That's what I do when I write it down. And even though I know that it won't change anything, it makes me feel a lot better.

When I grow up, I plan to be a writer at *DUH!*, where I know my mouth droppings and razor-sharp wit will finally be understood and I can stop hearing about being a normal girl. But until then, I'll be recording the stuff that bugs me in a new notebook my mom just bought me. She said that since she won't be here when I start school, I should "vent" in the notebook. I keep my vent-book in my desk drawer.

Someday the world will appreciate it.

Vent #1: Is it normal to be normal?

Who decides what's normal, anyway? How come we never see any pictures of the people who make up definitions for the word "normal" in dictionaries, huh? Is it because they look weird? And have they ever tried saying "normal" really fast over and over again? It sounds like a crew member's name on <u>Star Trek</u>.

I always thought that normal is supposed to mean different things to different people, right? Except for some reason, that doesn't apply to girls. A normal girl is supposed to act polite, cheerful, and easy to get along with. Let me say right now that no one could-or would-ever use one of those words to describe me. As for looking like a normal girl (which generally means how your mother would like you to dress: in neat, stylish clothes, with some-but not too much-makeup), I figure, why bother, since I don't act like a normal girl, anyway. If people met a girl who was dressed in a cute matching outfit but was loud, grumpy, and sarcastic, they might wonder if they've been transported to a parallel universe.

Sounds like a nice place to live.

CHAPTER THREE

It was my first day of school, before homeroom, and I was in the girls' bathroom. I stared at the light putrid green wall with MR. BARTON IS A HUNK! written on it. I was compelled to uncap a highlighter and scrawl underneath, A HUNK OF WHAT?

Sometimes I amaze even myself.

It was now 8:47. Three minutes until the bell rings. Taking a deep breath, I looked in the mirror. There was a person with medium-length dark hair, dressed in a ribbed white turtleneck, a black skirt, and (gasp) quasi-chunky black oxfords. The face was pale, the smallish mouth a little tense; only the hazel eyes looked . . . real. Let me summarize for those of you who are confused: I looked like a neat, nicely dressed, wholesome girl with her hair off her face, eager and enthusiastic to begin her first day of eighth grade in her exciting new school.

In other words, I was disguised as a normal girl.

That's right. I'll give you a moment to recover, maybe to get some Pepto-Bismol, because you did read that last bit correctly: I, Eve Belkin, looked like a normal girl in the mirror of the middle school.

Let me explain.

It was before breakfast on the first day at my new school. I was in a clothing crisis. How did I want to look when I walked into my classroom and thirty faces gaped at me like I was a piece of greenish baloney? Picking up my jeans, I tried to determine at what angle the hole in the seat exposed my underwear. But then I heard something. A yell and a crash from the kitchen. I ran downstairs in my nightgown.

I found my dad with his hand under the cold-water tap, the cast-iron pan of scrambled eggs on the floor. Mom was rummaging around in her suitcase, making sure for the hundredth time that she had everything. David, my alleged brother, was standing at the counter, guzzling orange juice out of the carton.

"Why didn't you tell me about that pan?" said my dad, patting his hand with a towel. "I thought they didn't make pans with handles that get hot anymore."

"I told you to take a hot pad, Peter, but you weren't listening," said my mother, snapping her suitcase shut. "I'm sorry that I can't take you to school today, Evie."

"That's okay, Mom," I lied.

"I know you'll do fine," she said.

"Mom wanted to show me how to make oatmeal, but what's to show?" piped up Dad, chuckling. "You put in some oats, you put in some water, you heat it up, and voila, you have oatmeal."

My mom smiled, but I could tell she was worried about leaving us.

"There's a copy of my itinerary on the refrigerator, honey, " she said as she finished her coffee. "Please call me if there are any problems."

David belched, opened a blueberry Pop-Tart, dropped the wrapper on the floor, and started toward the door. He grabbed his jacket, said something incomprehensible while spraying Pop-Tart crumbs, waved, and left.

"What problems?" asked Dad. "No problems, here. Right, kiddo? No problems at all."

He looked at me with a smile and a thumbs-up sign. How I hate those stupid thumb signs. I wanted to tell my father how trite, how meaningless, how *clichéd* his gesture was. But I decided that he might not appreciate my insight right now. I forced my thumb into an upward position for an eighth of a second.

"See, Ann? We're a team," crowed Dad. "I've already talked to Eve. She's going to turn over a new leaf. And now that I think of it, so am I. It's Eve's first day at school and it's my first day on my new job as househusband. Two new leaves, in the same house!"

That was when Mom turned around and gave me a look. No, not just a regular look, but a long, steady look that said: *Take care of your father. Make sure he's okay. Don't let him know if he screws up. I'm counting on you.*

She came over, kissed me on the top of the head, and left.

My mother had talked to me last night about Dad's "self-esteem" and his "identity crisis." She said that Dad had devoted almost every waking hour to that "unmentionable" car company and might not do things very efficiently around the house at first. We had to be patient and understanding with him. We had to make sure everything went smoothly while he "redefined his new role" in the family. We were all to pitch in and help him keep the house in order. It would greatly help, she added, if I could have a "positive attitude" and try to "get along" with the teachers and kids at my new school.

In other words, on top of everything else, I should stop being "difficult" and start acting like a "normal" girl.

"Normal girls" have girlfriends. They hang out in the "normal girl" clique at school. They are interested in "normal girl stuff" like clothes, hair, makeup, boys, etc. They don't have mouth droppings.

My first act as a normal girl and my father's protector was a challenging one: how not to gag at the breakfast table. When I attempted to eat, my spoon practically ricocheted off the oatmeal my dad had made for me. Upon further inspection I discovered that it was not, in fact, oatmeal as we know it. It was, in fact, one enormous oatmeal *lump*. But I, the new-leaved, normal Eve, was not going to go, "EUW! Gross!" No, the new Eve slipped the giant lump secretly into her napkin, then went upstairs to get dressed.

When I came back down, Dad was sitting at the table reading the want ads. He was hunched over and a lock of his salt-and-pepper hair hung down in his face. His hair had gotten saltier over the last few months. I supposedly resembled him. Since people always told me that I had the kind of regular face that could go pretty or not (I checked every day to see how it was going), I guess that Dad had the same kind of face. I thought he was handsome, though, especially when he shaved.

Reading the want ads was our father-daughter morning ritual; I was addicted to them. "Here's something, Dad." I pointed to a little box. "'Plasma Donor. No experience needed. Must be healthy.' That sounds promising."

He was quiet for a minute, then pushed his chair back and stood up.

"Nope! No more want ads for me. I have a new job, remember?" He picked up the paper and tossed it in the recycling bin.

I was getting so sick of his little, quote, job, unquote, I wanted to scream. But instead I opened the refrigerator to grab something for lunch. "Dad, it looks like we're running out of milk," I mentioned helpfully.

Dad didn't answer; he was looking at a flyer that had fallen out onto the floor.

"Dad?"

He looked up.

"We're almost out of milk," I repeated.

"I'll pick up some later."

"What are you going to do today?" I asked, sticking some crackers in my backpack.

"Well, I thought first I'd caulk some windows and maybe fix that dripping faucet in the bathroom, plus the garage needs cleaning out and the car could use a waxing."

"What are you going to make for dinner?"

"Dinner?" He swatted his hand at me. "Oh, who knows. It's no big deal; I can whip something up in fifteen minutes."

"But you've never made dinner before," I pointed out. "Do you know how to cook?"

He laughed. "Of course I do! Everyone knows how to cook, silly!" Suddenly he put his hand on his chest and gasped dramatically. "Eve! What are you wearing? You look so nice."

Even though I knew I was going to hear this when my father saw me in my "nice" clothes, I still couldn't stand it. If you're a girl, people constantly remark on your appearance. Why? No one tells boys they look nice; as long as boys don't have dried relish stuck to their pants, they look nice.

I sighed as I got my backpack and opened the front door, shielding my eyes from the sun. Just to get on my nerves, it was a beautiful day where everything outside seemed clear and bright—just the kind of day to turn over a new you-know-what.

Vent #2: Being yourself (yeah, right).

Just "be yourself," everyone tells you. But being yourself is different for boys than for girls. Being yourself for a boy means wearing the same underwear for three months; being yourself for a girl means ... who knows?

That's because for a girl to be herself she has to decide how she wants to look. And when it comes to deciding how you want to look, being a boy is a million times easier.

Why, you may ask. Well, first of all, any way you look as a girl says something about you. If you think: I don't care, I'm not doing anything about the way I look, people assume that that says something about you like, "Eve is wearing blue jeans that are missing a seat and a sweatshirt with holes under the arms and her hair is in her face and her toes are sticking up through her shoes, which means that she doesn't care about how she looks, so she will never have a boyfriend or get married or have children and will sponge off her parents forever."

I think it's totally unfair that girls have to worry so much about how they look. If I ruled the world I would order all kids to wear gray baggy uniforms that make everyone look exactly the same regardless of race, creed, color, and whatever else that line says. Then you could <u>really</u> be yourself.

CHAPTER FOUR

It was third period English. I found my class and hurled myself into an empty seat. So far my first day as a normal girl had been uneventful; I hadn't talked much to anyone and no one had talked to me. Although I was treated to the greenish-baloney gaze when I first walked into homeroom, I pretended to be absorbed in an old *DUH!* magazine that I had packed for this exact purpose. At least the famous brain managed to be useful once in a while.

Since kids were still filing in, the teacher, Ms. Harley, came over and introduced herself. Her hair was a springy mass of reddish curls and she looked young and relentlessly perky, like she had just finished college. I could tell that she hadn't had the enthusiasm beaten out of her yet by a steady diet of obnoxious eighth graders. I smiled at her. By the end of the year, she'd be singing a different tune.

The class ambled in. Two girls sat down at my table. It was amazing luck because they were exactly what I needed for my plan: normal girls. On the normal scale, they were closer to the teen-girl-magazine types—dressed in trendy clothes and wearing more makeup—but in my outfit I wasn't too far off. One of the girls gave me a little smile; the other acted like I was lint. I thoughtfully gazed down at my notebook so Lint Queen could evaluate if I . . . had potential.

Ms. Harley clapped her hands like she was in kindergarten.

"Hi, everybody, and welcome back! I'm very happy to see you all. I hope you guys had a terrific vacation! Who got some great presents?" She widened her eyes and gazed excitedly around the room.

Nobody responded.

"Oh, you're all a bunch of Scrooges! Well, I hope you guys remembered your assignment over the break, which was to . . . ?"

"Write a poem," a few kids droned.

"Yes!" exclaimed Ms. Harley joyously. "Who wants to go first?"

Nobody responded. Ms. Harley frowned, crossed her arms, and tapped her foot like she was waiting for a three-year-old to stop finger painting on the wall.

"Now, come on, guys," she said as she looked over at a table of three boys who were snickering about something. "How about you, Brady?"

Brady sighed deeply and lumbered to his feet. He had a wide neck, a buzz cut, and was wearing a Dallas Cowboys sweatshirt. He ignored the boys around him and tried to look serious.

"Hooray, hooray, it's New Year's Day.
The college bowls will now be played.

Couch potatoes from far and near
Join together to sit on their rears.

"Here come the linebackers.
Look at them go,
They're pounding our quarterback
Into Jell-O.

"But now it's close.
I'm ready to cheer,
To shriek with joy
Or erupt into tears."

The boys near him clapped. Across the room, a boy with a bright green Mohawk burst into high laughter. Ms. Harley looked like she might cry.

"That was wonderful, Brady. We all get poetic inspiration from different sources. The 'College Bowls' brings out your full range of emotions. Very expressive and powerful poetry. Thank you."

Brady mumbled something and sat down. A boy next to him said, "Ooh, powerful, Brady." Brady socked him in the shoulder.

At my table, the nicer girl leaned over and whispered to the other one, "It's, like, such a turn-on to hear Brady say that he 'erupts into tears.' He's *soooo* sensitive. Don't you think?"

The other one, who was still acting like I was lint, rolled her eyes.

Ms. Harley looked around excitedly. "Who's next?

I can't wait to hear more!" A girl behind me raised her hand. "Lydia."

Lydia stood up, pulled at the rear of her black stretch pants, and smoothed down her tunic top. She took a deep breath and held her stomach in. At her table was a skinny kid with glasses and long dark hair. He gave her an encouraging smile. Lydia began in a soft voice.

"Junk food, oh, junk food, I can't stay away.
Popcorn and pretzels, I love Frito-Lay.
Cheese curls, beer nuts, mesquite-flavored chips,
Are ready and waiting to pass through my lips.

"Häagen-Dazs and Pepperidge Farm
Make me happy, keep me warm;
And though I try hard to resist
I must have just one Hershey's Kiss."

The skinny boy clapped; the two normal girls cracked up. Lydia gave them a withering look and sat down. Ms. Harley sounded trembly. "What truth! What honesty! Lydia, you've revealed your innermost self to us like a true poet!"

The friendlier girl whispered to the other, "Her outermost self is already, like, very revealed." The corners of Lint Queen's mouth turned up slightly.

Ms. Harley, ready to burst with happiness, pointed to the nicer girl at my table. "Kristen? Let's hear yours."

Kristen was small and petite with pretty blue eyes and slightly buck teeth. Her light brown hair was pulled back into a bun. She was wearing a miniskirt and a short sweater. She gave the other girl an embarrassed smile, bit her lower lip, and stood up.

> *"Let's go to the mall, the mall, the mall,*
> *Where the clothes are large, medium,*
>   *and small.*
> *I try on some pants*
> *Imported from France*
> *For my big date with hunky Paul."*

Lint Lady rolled her eyes again. Ms. Harley gave a little shriek of joy. Was she like this with all her classes? She must kick her dog when she gets home.

Lydia piped up. "A new Ben & Jerry's just opened at the mall. There's a new flavor called 'Treehugger Mint.'"

"There's a sale on cross-trainers at The Athlete's Foot," remarked Brady.

"The mall is a capitalist shrine for materialistic pagans," said a girl dressed all in black next to the kid with the green Mohawk.

"I like the way you varied the rhythms of your poem, Kristen," said Ms. Harley. "Your middle lines rhymed and the last line echoed back to the beginning ones. Very good." She paused. "And who, may I ask, is Paul?"

Kristen blushed. "Like, no one, actually. It just rhymed." She looked at me; I smiled back at her.

"Next?" asked Ms. Harley. "Lisle?"

So the one who was acting like I was lint was named Lisle. Like weasel? What kind of a name is that? Lisle started looking through her notebook. I took the opportunity to study her. She was tall and well developed, with high cheekbones and light blue eyes. She held her head high, and, with her arched eyebrows, looked like she either smelled something bad or was supremely bored. Her hair was blonde, long and thick, and she tossed it back dramatically.

"I forgot mine," she said, barely lifting her eyes to Ms. Harley.

"Okay," said Ms. Harley. "I want it tomorrow. No later."

Lisle rolled her eyes and gave Kristen a look. Kristen giggled.

Seth (Mohawk) and Vanessa (lady in black) were laughing about something at their table. Vanessa wore a small silver nose ring in addition to black lipstick, hair, nails, and clothing.

"Seth? Since you and Vanessa are enjoying class so much, why not share your poem with us?" asked Ms. Harley.

Seth stood up. His Mohawk was the color of kiwi fruit (the inside part). He read in a monotone:

"Darkness, blackness, emptiness, vastness
Surrounds and encompasses the nothingness
Of the void.
The air is despair.

I breathe it in
But I cough up desperation,
Loneliness and phlegm.
Nothing is black
And black is . . . nothing."

There was a long pause.

Vanessa nodded her head slowly. "Wow. Deep."

Kristen whispered, "Yuck, phlegm. Like, I'm going to hurl."

Brady snorted in disgust.

Ms. Harley turned to Seth. "Interesting, Seth, and very profound. You demonstrated to the class that a non-rhyming poem can sometimes better express one's feelings than a rhyming one. Very good."

Seth grunted and sat down.

"Bitchin'," said the boy with shoulder-length, bleached blond hair next to him. Even though it was fifteen degrees outside, he was wearing black latex biking shorts and a T-shirt that read, "And on the eighth day, God made a surfboard."

Ms. Harley looked at him. "That is not an appropriate adjective, Donny."

She glanced at the clock. "Well, time has really flown today with all these wonderful poems! I think we can hear one more." She pointed to the skinny kid who sat next to Lydia. "Ian."

Ian adjusted his glasses and tucked his long dark hair behind his ears. Lydia giggled a little as he began to read.

"When you see me don't head for the door
Because I'll explain H2SO4.
I'm the greatest math whiz that's ever been.
My grasp of numbers is Pythagorean.
I love lasers, transistors, and rocketry, too.
It gives me great joy—'cause I'm smarter
*   than you."*

The whole class laughed. Even Lisle.

"You all did beautifully with your poems, people," said Ms. Harley in that gushing tone teachers get when they think they've really gotten to their students. "I want you to give yourselves a round of applause."

Lisle rolled her eyes again. Seth and Vanessa booed. Brady whistled. Everyone else managed to clap a few times. Kristen looked at Lisle and rolled her eyes, too.

Then they both looked at me. Eye contact—especially from Lisle—meant that they were considering me. This was the big moment. They were waiting for a sign that I wanted to join them.

The normal-girl plan had worked.

But then I realized that I'd have to follow a girl who acted like I was lint. To survive, I'll have to do some major venting, I thought as I sat there looking down at my notebook. Should I really go through with this for my dad and mom?

But as I asked myself that question, I knew I was being dishonest. The normal-girl plan wasn't only for my parents; *I* was tired of being difficult, tired of acting like being witty was better than having friends, tired of pretending that all I needed for company was my *DUH!* magazine.

I looked at Kristen and Lisle.

And rolled my eyes.

CHAPTER FIVE

I realized I was actually whistling as I walked up the driveway to my house after school. The car was gone, which meant my dad wasn't home. I was disappointed; I'd wanted to tell him about Lisle and Kristen. If Mom was here, she'd be at the door, waiting to hear how everything went on my first day.

I walked into the kitchen and blinked. Nothing had been touched since I left at 8:00 this morning. I didn't remember Mom ever leaving dirty dishes for more than . . . fifteen minutes. I'd always thought she was a little ridiculous. But now, as I discovered the pot of hardened, solidified oatmeal and the melted dish of margarine next to it, I decided to rethink my position.

But starting today, I was now mature and helpful, and undaunted by gross leftover breakfast food. I put away the milk and margarine and ran some hot water in the fossilized oatmeal pot. After a little while, I heard my dad pull up in the driveway. He was whistling as he came into the kitchen, carrying six large grocery bags.

"Eve!" he exclaimed, like he had forgotten that I lived here.

"Hi, Dad. Where were you?"

He sat down at the table, shoving the dirty dishes out of his way. "At the store," he answered. "How was school?"

"Pretty good." I picked up the dishes from the table and carried them over to the sink.

"That's great, honey," he said, opening a bag.

I leaned over and opened the dishwasher and waited for him to ask me more about my day, the way my mother would. But he didn't. Out of the corner of my eye I spotted something. The bags that Dad was holding weren't from SuperFoods like I'd first thought, they were from somewhere else.

"What's HomePro? A new store?"

"Yep," he said excitedly. "A great new store. I spent most of my day there." He reached in a bag and pulled out an electric drill.

"What, Dad? I can't hear you too well over the noise of the dishes," I yelled, not too subtly, I suppose. But it was okay, because he didn't get it.

"Evie, this store is terrific." He raised his voice and came up next to me at the sink but was not conscious of what I was actually doing there. "It's a huge do-it-yourself store that has everything, every single thing you need to fix up your house. If you want to build an addition or insulate an attic or redo a bathroom, they have videotapes of how to do it, step-by-step. And the people who work there! Incredibly friendly and helpful. They knew every question I was going to ask even before *I* did!"

I reached past him for the coffeepot and knocked over some orange juice on his drill.

"Hey," he said, "watch it." He took the sponge and tenderly wiped off the drill.

And then I glanced down at a large paperback book on the table and felt a cold chill come over me. The title was *Do It Yourself: A Guide to Building an Outdoor Deck.*

He saw me reading it. "Well? What do you think? Great idea, huh?"

Luckily, my back was turned so I had a minute to decide how to react. I had no idea if this was a great idea or not. If I had to bet, though, I'd go for the "not."

"What's a great idea?" I asked innocently.

"A deck, silly! An outdoor deck. Like this one right here." He pointed to the picture on the front of the book. "I've decided that's just what we need for this house." He was smiling. I didn't think that I'd seen him look that happy for a long time.

"I'm ready to get to work," he said, enthusiastically unloading stuff out of the bags. "The salesman said that all you needed to put in was about two hours of work a day and you'd be finished in two months. I figure that since I'll be able to work eight hours a day on it, I should be done in a couple of weeks."

I nodded, glancing over at the little piece of memo

paper on the refrigerator door. Mom had made a long list of things that needed to be done during the week. Today was Tuesday, garbage day. Dad had forgotten to take the cans out. Under that list was a grocery list; Dad hadn't done that, either. Under that list was a laundry schedule; David, the sweat king, needed a lot of clean gym clothes. And now that I was a normal girl I couldn't wear my jeans for two weeks anymore without washing them.

Dad noticed me looking at the refrigerator. "What? That list?" He made a swatting gesture with his hand. "I'm too busy to worry about those things right now. And besides, you and I always thought Mom worried too much about things like that, remember?"

He walked out of the room, chuckling. Yeah, I remembered. But it was somehow different when Mom was here. The kitchen table was now full of cans of varnish, drills, saws, books, hammers, the newspaper want ads, cups, dishes, and . . . a bar of Lava soap. That's right. You read correctly.

Lava soap.

Vent #3: An electric drill in Marry-Me Mauve, please.

I wonder if my dad feels the same way at HomePro as I do when I walk through Kogan's cosmetics department. All those lipsticks and lip liners and lip glosses and blush-ons and eye shadows and mascaras and toners and loofahs and night creams and exfoliating scrubs have evil powers. You're on your way to the bathroom and your eye falls upon rows of shimmering smudge sticks. Their existence on this earth means only one thing: that you need help. They're calling your name. Loudly. You slow down. You cannot resist. Next to the smudge sticks is a sleek black lipstick with the word "Tester" on the side. It's just like <u>Alice in Wonderland</u> when Alice finds the bottle that says "Drink Me." You must test it. It is your destiny. As you reach for it, a salesperson appears behind the counter. She looks fabulous. She smiles and you know she's thinking, "Yes. Another sucker."

I think that when my dad walks into a store like HomePro, he must feel the same way. The hammers whisper, the saws beckon, the pliers plead, and the poor guy can't resist. He hardly knows what to do with any of this stuff, but it makes him nervous. What is all this? Do other people know how to use it? If it's here, I must need it. Then a smiling salesperson appears behind the rows of insulation material. He's wearing a manly looking apron. He has a pencil behind his ear. He thinks, "Yes. Another sucker."

We are helpless against the forces of evil.

CHAPTER SIX

"Hello?"

"Hi, honey. It's me."

"Mom!"

"How did it go today on the first day of school?"

"Uh, okay."

"Anyone seem, dare I say it, nice? Or even . . . friendly?"

I decided not to tell her about Lisle and Kristen right now.

"Everyone seemed . . . okay."

She laughed. "That's my Evie. Brimming with optimism and positive as always. Is anything ever better than okay?"

"Not when my mother isn't here to see me off on my first day." A mouth dropping. I shouldn't have said it.

She sighed. "Oh, come on, Eve, that's not fair. We talked about all of this, right? Remember the new family roles? Helping your father out? Being more responsible and mature?"

"Yeah, I know." It was hard to keep remembering that Dad's problems right now were worse than mine. Even harder for my mouth.

"Anyway, I knew you'd be fine today and you were," she continued. "Wasn't Dad home after school?"

"Eventually. But I had to clean up the breakfast dishes."

"No! You're kidding!" She responded with mock horror. "The dishes? You?"

"I know it's not a big deal, Mom, but isn't Dad supposed to do that? You would never let the dishes from breakfast sit around all day."

She took a deep breath. "You're right and you complained that I was 'neurotic' about keeping the kitchen clean, right?"

"Well . . ."

"You know, Eve, there are lots and lots of families where kids not only wash the dishes but cook and clean and run laundry because both parents are working. You and David and Dad are all going to run the house together. It's a team effort, remember? Please don't start whining about the situation now."

"I wasn't whining," I said angrily. "I was just stating a fact." Whining is a touchy subject since I've frequently been accused of it in the past. I sat on the phone for a few moments not saying anything.

"Look, honey, I don't want to fight. I just want you to help Dad out—that's all. We are all trying to get used to these changes."

I sighed. "I know. Don't worry. I will help him."

"That's my girl. Just be patient with Dad. It'll get easier, I promise. Could I speak to him now?"

"Sure. Bye, Mom. I love you."

"I love you too, Evie. I'll call you in a few days."

I put the phone down and called Dad. I had, what you would call, a sense of foreboding.

It did not feel good.

CHAPTER SEVEN

It was a few days later, the end of math class, fifth period. Stone-Age Mrs. Henry was giving us a pop quiz to "see if our brains had deteriorated from inactivity and rum-laced fruitcake over the Christmas vacation." I thought that was funny until she asked me if I thought she was a stand-up comedian and I had to admit, no, although in my opinion, she had potential. This was very close to being a mouth dropping, which I couldn't afford if I wanted to be accepted. The Lisle group expanded sometimes to include other girls, but Kristen was a constant. And, of course, Lisle was always the queen.

Luckily, for me, however, the pop quiz was algebra, which happened to be one of my best subjects. I finished earlier than anybody, which gave me a good opportunity to dissect everyone else.

I watched as Lydia unwrapped a Hershey's Hug between her thighs and popped it into her mouth. Brady, the jock, was hunched over his desk, chin in hand, eyes staring straight ahead. Maybe he figured that if he sat in the "Thinker" pose, he would, in fact, think. Seth was also hunched over his desk, twirling some pieces of his Mohawk in concentration.

Then something on the floor caught my eye: a backpack with a *DUH!* sticking out of it. It was number 423, from 1996, one of my favorite issues. I strained my neck to see who it belonged to. Then Ian leaned over and stuffed it into his loose-leaf to hide it under his desk. He had finished the quiz already, too.

I heard some whispering off to the side and saw Kristen angling her test paper so Lisle could copy off it. Lisle was motioning to Kristen to lift it up. Kristen gave a worried glance toward Mrs. Henry, who was writing something at her desk, then lifted her paper up. Vanessa, who sat behind Kristen, gave a disgusted snort. Mrs. Henry looked up.

"Is something wrong, Vanessa?"

Vanessa didn't answer.

"Did you wish to say something or were you just making unladylike noises?" asked Mrs. Henry.

Vanessa looked at Mrs. Henry and then at Lisle. It was completely quiet in the room. Kristen had turned pale; Lisle was calmly doodling hearts on her paper.

Vanessa narrowed her eyes. "What is a ladylike noise, Mrs. Henry?"

I sucked in some air. Go, Vanessa!

"I will not tolerate back talk in my class, Vanessa," snapped Mrs. Henry. "You've earned a trip to Mrs. Fletcher's office."

Vanessa gave her a nasty look, gathered up her books, and started to leave. At the door she stopped and turned around.

"Since cheating makes no noise, it's more ladylike. Right, Lisle?"

Lisle didn't miss a beat; her pen didn't even hesitate on the drawing of her hearts. She had no problem letting Vanessa take the blame for her. Vanessa stomped out of the door. Mrs. Henry looked at Lisle.

"Lisle, do you have anything to tell me?"

Lisle shook her head slightly, her eyes downcast under the high eyebrows.

"I find it hard to believe that a girl like you would cheat," Mrs. Henry said, starting to collect the quizzes. "Others, however, I'm not so sure about."

Why? I wondered. But no sooner did I have the thought than the answer came rushing upon me. Of course! What Mrs. Henry really meant was that she found it hard to believe that a girl who *looked* like Lisle would cheat. A girl who was wearing a kilt and matching twin-sweater set did not fit her idea of a cheater. But a girl dressed in black with skeleton dangly earrings? She would cheat *and* make false accusations.

The bell rang and we filed out. I was walking near Lisle when Kristen grabbed her arm from behind.

"Lisle, I can't believe what just happened," she said breathlessly.

Lisle, walking quickly, merely shrugged.

"But, like, Vanessa saw us!" exclaimed Kristen. "What if she says something to Mrs. Fletcher?"

We had reached our lockers. Kristen looked stricken. I felt bad, too, but I didn't dare say anything.

"Lisle, maybe we should go to Mrs. Fletcher's, maybe Vanessa hasn't seen her yet?"

Lisle gave her a look of irritation and calmly worked her combination lock. When she finally spoke her voice was so quiet, we had to strain to hear it. "Who is Mrs. Fletcher going to believe: Vampira or me?"

"But, but, uh—" Kristen stuttered.

"Get over it, Kristen. Nothing's going to happen to us," muttered Lisle.

Kristen backed away to her locker. I was ready to go to mine when Lisle grabbed my arm. She rolled her eyes toward Kristen and smiled slyly.

"Are you a math genius or something?"

I shrugged.

"You were done first. Even before Ian, the dork. Kristen's not bad, but she sometimes misses a few." She looked me straight in the eye. "I've always thought it would be *soooo* hard to leave all your friends and move to a new school. But you're lucky; at least you don't have to worry about math." She paused. "Maybe next time you'll help me out."

So being in the Lisle clique had a price.

"Come on," said Lisle. "Let's walk to the bus together."

She grabbed my arm and started down the hall. Kristen banged her locker shut and ran to catch up with us. We linked arms, with Lisle in the center, and marched down the school steps. It felt fun, yet phony at the same time.

The normal-girl plan that was supposed to make my life easier was already getting complicated. I guess I—yes, owner of the famous brain—hadn't thought about what being in this group really meant. It meant that you could get kicked out of the group in a nanosecond if you didn't do what Lisle wanted. Then you'd be exiled to teenage-girl Siberia, where no one ever had a good hair day.

Where the old me used to live.

Vent #4: With liberty and buzz cuts for all.

Here's how I feel about hair: I'm jealous of boys who have buzz cuts. Okay, these days girls can have a buzz cut, too, but it's certainly not considered normal. I, for example, could not easily get one, while my brother has had a buzz for years. I can only imagine the joy of not having to deal with hair. You can wash it in twelve seconds. Just take the bar of Dial and scrub your head. No combing, brushing, gelling, moussing, fixing, nothing. It's dry before you've even grabbed your towel. It's neat, it doesn't get in the way of anything, and you never have to hear that if you moved your hair off your face then people could see how pretty you are. You don't need to worry about pretty because you're a boy.

But the best thing about a buzz cut is that the wearer is not responsible for how he looks. When you have a buzz cut, all that's left is your face. That's it. If you're good-looking and you have a buzz cut, great. If you're ugly, well, tough. And tough for the rest of the world because the kid with the buzz cut doesn't have to look at himself—<u>we</u> do. With a buzz cut, your head's out there, alone. If it's the size of a raisin and your ears stick out like doorknobs, well, the rest of the world can just lump it.

Now imagine a girl whose ears stick out like doorknobs. She would devote her life to trying to find a hairstyle that covers them so that the rest of the world will never know her terrible secret. That's what she would be expected to do. Also, she would talk about her problem with her friends, asking for advice like should she comb her hair forward or back or wear a headband or does she need more mousse or a perm or something. She would never, _ever_, dream of cutting her hair short.

I think that we should all get buzz cuts to go with our gray baggy uniforms.

CHAPTER EIGHT

"Here," my dad said, handing me two six-pound cans of tomatoes. "Let's take a few of these. I'm running out of room in my cart."

I sighed. It was after school, and we were grocery shopping, buying enough bulk foods to feed several Third World countries.

"Dad, we don't need two cans. It's way too much," I said, knowing it wouldn't matter.

He ignored me and started piling stuff into my cart: an eight-pound can of fruit cocktail, a seven-pound container of Parmesan cheese, two six-pound cans of kidney beans.

"I don't want to have to keep making trips to the grocery store. I have other, more important, work to do around the house," he said, rearranging the ten-pound bag of elbow macaroni. "Look around. There are hardly any people shopping in the middle of the afternoon. I want to get plenty of food and then back to work."

I sighed.

"Besides," he went on, "it's silly to buy small cans when you can get so much more for your money.

With these tomatoes, I'll make some spaghetti sauce tomorrow. Or—" he snapped his fingers like he had a great idea "—chili! I made killer chili when I was in college."

"But, Dad, these sizes are for the army or something. I don't think you need that much."

"And I'm pretty sure I have a coupon for the Parmesan cheese," he said, stopping to shuffle his coupons around.

"That's great. We'll use some on your killer spaghetti and then send the rest to the marines."

"It's killer *chili* and I'm pretty sure I also have a coupon for . . . yep, here it is . . . eight boxes of Luigi's lasagna noodles."

"Dad," I said wearily, "no one likes lasagna. I don't like it and neither does David." I thought for a minute. "And neither do *you*. You don't like lasagna. Remember?"

He shook his finger at me. "Oh, that doesn't mean anything. You don't need to use lasagna noodles just for lasagna. That's the problem with you guys; you don't think about food creatively. With lasagna noodles you can make nachos or egg rolls or . . . pancakes! And besides, this stuff keeps forever." He moved some stuff around in the cart. "Eve, grab that jumbo-size box of instant mashed potatoes. Look, there's a special on split peas. Do you think we need another cart, honey?"

I moved away. I suddenly had an impulse to smack him in the head with a bag of manicotti. Was this how normal, everyday people were driven to commit murder?

Then I noticed all the people shopping near us were watching us. Gee, I wonder why? Maybe it was because Dad and I each had a cart and we were pulling two more. Maybe it was because we were having an argument at each new item. Maybe it was because this was the shopping trip from hell. We had been in the grocery store for forty-five minutes; we were still in Aisle 1, Economy Sizes.

I left my dad and the carts and took a little walk around the salad bar to calm down. I didn't think grocery shopping could be so . . . embarrassing. When I went shopping with my mom I would help her if she needed help, but she usually didn't. She was done in an hour or so. Our cart looked like everyone else's. She never dragged another cart behind her or asked me to take one.

Suddenly I heard my name over the loudspeaker. "Would Eve Belkin please go to the dairy products, please? Eve Belkin, dairy products."

I ran to the dairy products. My dad was loading a case of Parkay margarine into his cart.

"What! What?" I exclaimed, running up to him. "What's the matter?"

He looked up at me, annoyed. "Where have you been, Eve? I'm trying to shop and I turn around and you're gone. Where were you?"

"I always walk around when I'm with Mom," I said, looking around at the faces staring at us. "Geez, Dad. I'm not a baby."

"I thought you were supposed to help me here," he continued. "Didn't you say that you help Mom when she shops?"

"I was trying to help you, Dad, but you weren't listening to me," I explained. "I told you we didn't need those giant cans and jars of stuff. Mom never buys that size of anything."

"And Mom spends a lot of time and money," he replied. "I'm trying to think of family meals that give us more for our money. Is there something wrong with that?"

I shook my head. This was a losing battle. I reminded myself to be more patient and understanding with Dad, but I wished my mother had been more explicit. Am I allowed to disagree with him? What if I think he's doing something wrong?

And who do I go to with my complaints?

But, suddenly, I was jolted from my thoughts. Like a bad plot twist in a horror movie, I heard my name again. This time from around Aisle 6, Health and Beauty Aids. Someone I knew was calling me. And suddenly there was Kristen, coming around the corner, a little red plastic carrying basket balanced on her wrist.

"Like, I heard your name over the loudspeaker," she said, coming up to me. In her little basket was some Yoplait yogurt, Pepperidge Farm Milano cookies, and SnackWell fat-free graham crackers. "What ha—"

But she didn't finish her sentence because she was staring at my cart. Carts. Plural. At the contents of my carts. I let go of them like they were on fire. But it was too late. She had a very puzzled expression on her face and I knew what she was thinking: Normal girls don't buy sixty-four-ounce boxes of BuyRite pancake mix. I had to tap all my creative juices to get out of this one. I glanced around for my dad; luckily, he was off to the side, arguing with a stock boy who told him the special on the ten-pound block of Velveeta was over.

"What's all that stuff for?" she asked.

"What stuff?"

"That stuff!" She pointed at my carts. "Weren't you just holding those carts a minute ago?"

"*OOOOh!* You mean this stuff? In the cart?"

She nodded.

"It's food for . . . the homeless," I said, lowering my voice to give the word extra significance and make sure that my father didn't hear. Kristen's eyes widened. This was a gamble and as the seconds went by in silence I wasn't sure if it was the right one. Finally she spoke.

"That's"—she struggled to find the words—"*soooo* nice of you."

Whew. "Yeah. I take this to a soup kitchen downtown," I replied with a perfect combination of sadness (at the tragedy) and sacrifice (at how great I was). But, of course, I was now feeling extra guilty using homeless people in my lie.

"A real soup kitchen?" asked Kristen, looking confused. "But, don't they just, like, have soup?"

I smiled sadly and shook my head. "No. We try

to make all sorts of things. So they can have some variety."

She nodded solemnly. She understood. From my side vision I could see the stock boy coming out of a door straining under the weight of several Velveeta blocks. I had to hurry.

"Well, Kristen, I have to go." I gave her a serious look. "I can't be late."

"Oh, no. Don't be late." She starting backing up. "Like, maybe, I could help you there one day."

"Sure," I said, now pushing my carts proudly. "They'll take all the help they can get."

A car was honking outside. Kristen turned and waved. "I gotta go. See you tomorrow, Eve."

I waved and looked around for my dad. He was in a nearby checkout line. I could barely see him over the mountain of jumbo Wonder Bread packages on the counter. I got behind him and began hauling out my cans with a big sigh of relief. I'd managed to get out of that one using a big fat lie but if it had been Lisle . . . Well, just the thought of it made me shiver.

And now I realized another aspect about being in the normal-girl group. The normal standards went beyond you and your new nail polish: Your entire family had to fit the normal standards.

Somehow, I knew that Mr. Mom wouldn't make it.

CHAPTER NINE

"Hello?"

"Hi, honey. It's me."

"Mom! How's your trip going?"

"Great! My orders are way up!"

I tried to sound cheerful even though part of me—a very small part, okay?—was distressed to hear this news. "That's . . . great."

"I know. Some of my old customers told me how much they missed me. I couldn't believe they even remembered me!"

"That's great, Mom. Really."

"So." She paused for a second. "You're uncharacteristically quiet tonight, Evie. How are things going? How's Dad? How's school? Everything okay?"

"Yep. Dad's fine. Everything's okay." In my determination not to have a mouth dropping, I suddenly had an unpleasant realization: If I didn't complain about something or other, I . . . didn't have much to talk about.

Mom was happy, though.

"That's great!" she said. "How's David?"

This was my moment to point out that David was not on our keeping-the-house-clean team. But that would have been complaining.

"David's fine."

"Has Dad been cooking? What did he make for dinner tonight?"

"Uh, uh, uh . . . chili." We'd gone out for pizza.

"Chili?"

"Yeah. It was good."

"It was?"

"Yeah. I had two helpings." Now I was becoming a pathological liar, on top of my many, many other problems.

"Your dad made terrible chili in college. Maybe he followed a new recipe."

I had to control my laughter. "Maybe."

"I never thought you liked chili."

"Yeah, I don't. I mean, no, I do."

"Well, good. I'm glad. In fact, I'm thrilled that Dad is cooking food that you like. And tell me about school. Everything still just okay?"

I figured it was time to make her day. "It's good, actually. I met some girls who seemed nice."

"*What?* Did you just say what I thought you said? My daughter, the one who's allergic to the word 'nice?'" She lowered her voice. "Are you being sarcastic or not?"

"Hard to believe, but I'm not."

"What are they like?"

"Oh, I don't know. Just . . . normal girls."

"Well, I didn't think you would ever like 'just normal girls.' Maybe you've grown up a little, Evie."

"Yeah, maybe."

"You know, I'm relieved that everything is going well. Better, even, than I thought. See? I guess I don't give your dad enough credit."

"I guess not."

"Good. Well, please tell Dad I called to say hello and I'm pleased he's doing such a good job and that I'll talk to him soon."

"Okay."

"Love you, honey. Take care."

"Bye, Mom."

I put down the phone.

I had another realization: I was now a deeply superficial person.

CHAPTER TEN

We were at the mall, the mall, the mall, in a dressing room that was small, small, small. Kristen was trying on a pair of white vinyl pedal pushers. Lisle and I were wedged in the corners. Outside the curtain and peeking in were Trina and Deirdre, two other friends of Lisle's.

"So, like, what do you think?" Kristen looked nervously to Lisle for her approval.

We all waited.

"Ummmm. I guess they look good," said Lisle.

"You think so?" asked Kristen. "You don't think my butt looks, like, humongous?"

Lisle shook her head. Deirdre and Trina shook their heads.

"In fact," Lisle pondered, "they're almost baggy. Your butt looks skinny."

"So, do you, like, think it's too skinny?" asked Kristen.

We waited.

"No," said Lisle. "It's good skinny. I can still see your butt moving."

"Me, too," said Deirdre, who was short and wore glitter eye shadow.

51

"M-m-me, too," piped up Trina, who was tall, had a stutter, and wore brown lipstick.

"But is it, like, good to see your butt moving?" asked Kristen.

"Yes! But it shouldn't jiggle around a lot, like Jell-O," answered Lisle.

"Oh, great, now mine's, like, too skinny *and* jiggles around too much!" squealed Kristen.

Lisle got up and stretched. "Chill out, Kristen," she said. "We'll wait outside for you."

Lisle headed over to a counter with hats. She tried on a buckskin cowboy hat.

"That looks great on you," said Deirdre. "I'm too short to wear hats. Short people don't look good in hats."

"The W-W-Western look is really hot," said Trina.

I picked up a baseball cap and tried it on. Lisle looked at me.

"What do you think, Eve? How do you think this hat looks on me?"

By this time, I knew what she wanted to hear from me. "I'm not crazy about it."

"Why?"

"You're not the Western type," I explained.

Lisle came over and put her arm around me. "See? Eve is the only one who's not afraid to tell me the truth. Now, that's a true friend."

It was the end of January and we all had our group roles: Kristen (and Trina and Deirdre when they joined us) was the Lisle worshiper. I was too, of course, but not as much. I didn't actually disagree with her, but I didn't chime in quite as fast as the others. (As a result, I was known as the "quiet" one, a description that would've caused my family endless hysterics.)

I could tell by the contemptuous way Lisle treated the worshipers that she enjoyed having someone around who wasn't her toady all the time. She liked a bit of a challenge (emphasis on the *bit*). So I became that one, knowing that not being her toady all the time also meant she didn't trust me as completely as the others.

Lisle handed me a beige fedora. I tried it on. We both laughed at how dumb I looked.

"So when do we get to see your house?" she asked casually, tilting a black beret.

"That looks nice on you," I remarked, marveling that my voice was steady. I knew that this development was inevitable, and it filled me with fear. There was no way that Lisle could come over.

"So, when?" she persisted. "I'm thinking about having a sleepover next weekend, but I can't have someone sleep over whose room I haven't seen." She did a little playful pout. "What if your room is nicer than mine?"

I licked my lips. "I'm sure it's not and anyway, my room is still a mess from moving. There're boxes all over the place."

"So? Big deal," she replied.

"And—" It was obvious that I had to tell her something. The more I stalled, the further she pushed. I debated what would do the least damage: A mother who works isn't unusual; it's the father who doesn't do *anything* that's the problem. "I'm not allowed to have anyone over after school because I'm usually there by myself."

"Why?" she asked instantly. "Does your mother work?"

I nodded.

"What does she do?"

"She's in um, um, in the . . . medical field," I stammered.

Kristen walked up, holding her new pants. "Well, I got them. But I can return them tomorrow if the mirror in the dressing room was, like, distorted or something."

I tried to change the subject before she got around to my father's work. "My brother just got a job at a fancy health club called BadBods."

"Omigod!" shrieked Deirdre. "Did you say that your brother works at BadBods?"

I nodded. At least this was true.

"Wow. They only hire hunks there," Deirdre said to the others. "He has to be hunky. How old is he? Is he short?"

"D-d-does he look like you?" asked Trina.

"What's his job there?" asked Lisle.

"He's about six feet and I don't know if I look like him." I pretended not to hear Lisle's question. Not only did family members have to pass the normal standards, but their jobs did, too.

"W-w-what's his name?"

"David."

"Ooh, *verrrry* hunky name," said Kristen. "Like, when can we see him?"

"What's his job there?" asked Lisle, who was irritated at having to repeat her question.

"Um . . . he's a trainer." He'd wanted to get the job as personal trainer but wasn't qualified yet.

"A personal trainer?" said Lisle. "My parents play raquetball there. I'll have to ask them if they've met a new trainer."

I didn't say anything; I could always claim later that I didn't know he wasn't qualified for the job. The important thing was that she forgot, momentarily, about my father's job.

But I knew that with Lisle, *momentarily* was the key word.

I wanted to lay my weary head down on the hat counter and vent.

Vent #5: What a doll!

There are always a group of girls who seem to know more than you do. No, not about frog intestines or the square root of 589, but about mood makeovers, fake fur, and baby, baby tees. They can tell you that the pants you're wearing went out exactly twelve minutes and thirty-two seconds ago.

Most people would agree that girls like this have existed for eons. They are fashion experts and can tell you how to look if you're tending a herd of goats in Afghanistan one minute or finding the cure for cancer in the next.

Here's the important thing about these girls: It's not the styles that are really important, it's the idea that no matter what they do, they must always look stylish. So for example, when tending goats in Afghanistan, these girls would be wearing something like a Calvin Klein soft-as-butter, full-length pigskin skirt, ribbed, cotton fitted polo, distressed, country oxford hiking boots, and polarfleece hooded pullover.

But even then these girls would find something about their appearance that wouldn't be exactly right, exactly how they're supposed to look.

Which brings us to the <u>big question</u>: Who, exactly, are they supposed to look like?

Yes, there is a role model. And, yes, she <u>is</u> perfect. Absolutely. She never ever, <u>ever</u>, has a mega-zit or water weight or even one bad hair day. She has the amazing ability to become anything she wants to be and <u>always</u> look sexy, skinny, with big hair and great boobs. This is the fashion girls' goal. When they grow up these girls might want to be a TV host or a network anchor, or best of all, a supermodel. Their role model is all of these things . . . and more.

But she does have one flaw: She's twelve inches tall and made in Taiwan.

Can you guess yet?

It's . . . Barbie! These girls want to be human versions of Barbie dolls. Barbie looks skinny, sexy, and has big boobs in any situation! There's Neurosurgeon Barbie with her hot pink stethoscope and white doctor's coat (which she leaves unbuttoned because of her big boobs); and Power Business Lady Barbie in her black miniskirted suit and leopard vest (for when she takes her suit jacket off to unwind with Ken). Barbie may have an outfit for every job under the sun: Insurance Saleslady Barbie, Funeral Director Barbie, Rabbi Barbie.

And here is the weirdest part: The people who make Barbie think they are helping girls by having Barbie do all these fun jobs where she can wear stylish outfits. But really they're making things worse. So before, you would think, well, Barbie's a model or something that I could never be, but now if I want to herd goats in Afghanistan I still have to be skinny and have big boobs.

I say that if anyone in the world needs a baggy gray uniform outfit and a buzz cut, it's Barbie.

CHAPTER ELEVEN

On my way down the hall after English one day, I realized that I'd forgotten my notebook. I ducked my head back inside; Ms. Harley was at her desk.

"Excuse me, Ms. Harley, I left something in here."

She looked up and smiled. "No problem." Pause. "I'm glad to have a chance to talk."

Uh-oh.

"So," Ms. Harley said in that I-want-to-be-more-than-a-teacher-to-you voice. "Tell me, Eve, how is everything going for you here?"

"Okay."

She was now perched on the edge of my desk, tilting her head at me. "What kinds of books do you like to read?"

I shrugged. I wasn't sure what kinds of books were acceptable and I knew that Ms. Harley could easily blow my cover. "I don't know. Pretty much anything."

"Well, like what?" she asked, smiling. Her smile close up was making me squint.

I knew that I'd probably make this shorter and less painful if I just told her the truth . . . *some* truth.

"I like humor, comedy, that sort of thing," I muttered.

"Oh, me too!" she cried, jumping up and running to the bookshelf. "How about essays?"

"Well . . ." It didn't sound promising.

She handed me a large book, *The Collected Essays of Mark Twain*.

"Mark Twain?"

She nodded, her eyes bright with excitement. "Yes! Mark Twain was one of the funniest writers who ever lived."

"He was?"

"Absolutely! He hated hypocrisy and loved to make fun of the social customs of his day. His satiric essays are hilarious."

"They are?"

"Yes! Mark Twain knew that by showing the unfairness or illogic of something in a funny way, people would be able see it clearer."

That sure sounded a lot like . . . *DUH!* For one of the very few times in my life, I was speechless. I looked at the thick book in my hands.

"Thanks," I said. "When do you need it back?"

"Oh, keep it as long as you like," she answered. "After you read a few essays, maybe you'll think of something that really bugs you and you'll try your hand at one."

Stunned by that last remark (did she used to work on the *Psychic Home Shopping Network*?), I walked out the door.

"Bye, Eve, see you tomorrow."

I waved back and thought, if only Ms. Harley wouldn't smile so much, she'd be a lot more likable.

CHAPTER TWELVE

It was 10 P.M. several nights later and I'd just finished taking a shower. Stepping out of the bathtub, I put my wet foot on the floor and felt something ... unpleasant. I leaned against the wall, braced myself (psychologically), and looked at the sole of my foot. It was black with hair, dirt, and God only knows what else.

This was just the latest episode in the new scientific discovery series, *Emerging Forms of Life Inside Eve Belkin's House.* Today's discovery was "fur" growing on the bathroom floor that might, in time, merge with the mildew on the tile and create yet another new life form. A few days earlier I'd learned that if toothpaste is spit out into the sink and not rinsed down the drain in an hour or so, it will fossilize and stay there until archaeologists a thousand years from now discover it. I did finally figure out that by putting lots of water on it and scraping with your thumbnail, you can dislodge it. That is, of course, once you've gotten past the fact that it's someone else's toothpaste spit you're scraping.

I put on my nightgown, brushed my hair, and curled up with Mark Twain. Then I tried to decide if

I had the energy to scrounge up a snack. There was tons of food downstairs but . . . nothing to eat. After we'd bought our one hundred pounds of food during the shopping trip from hell, Dad made one batch of his killer chili and then forgot about the rest of his creative meal plans. In fact, starting something and then forgetting about it seemed to be keeping Dad really busy these days.

The deck was the first thing. On Monday, I got home from school and found him out there poring over his books, putting pencils behind his ear, and sharpening his drill. On Tuesday, he discovered a new plumbing supply place. He decided that the upstairs bathroom needed a complete overhaul, and now all the bathroom cabinets were lying on their sides in a row in the upstairs hallway. On Wednesday, he called from a kitchen remodeling place about twenty miles out of town and told me that he was at a "How to Update and Modernize Your Kitchen" session and he wouldn't be home for dinner. I didn't say, *excuuse me*, but, what dinner, because I was still trying to be patient and understanding.

When I'd ask Dad what about the deck, what about the bathroom, what about the lasagna pancakes (not to mention all the other stuff), I'd get the swatted-hand brush-off. It seemed that Dad had a different notion of what running the house meant. For him, it meant doing what he thought was "guy stuff" like home-improvement projects (or *starting* home-improvement projects). Things like cooking and cleaning didn't seem to count.

I was running some laundry and washing some dishes and picking up dirty clothes, but as far as I could tell, I was the only one doing anything. And even though I could be accused of whining, I didn't think it was fair. I thought my dad and brother should have been doing more, or at least something, but I didn't want to be "difficult," so I didn't say anything.

I tried to bring it up when my mom called earlier, but could barely get a word in edgewise: She was thrilled because she was selling more drugs than any other sales rep and her company was sending her to a special intensive training seminar. She asked if I'd be okay if she were gone a little longer. What could I say?

But the pressure from Lisle to see my house and meet my family wasn't going away. As time went on, it would only get worse. I might as well plaster it on a billboard: EVE BELKIN IS A FRAUD, OKAY? I hadn't realized that my house, my parents, their jobs, my brother, my dog, my *everything* was going to be judged by Lisle. And even though I knew this was ridiculous, that I shouldn't care about her opinion so much, I couldn't stop now. No one here knew me. These were my only "friends."

I sighed, put a bookmark in Mark Twain, and went downstairs. I had to admit that Ms. Harley was right about him; he was quite a venter. Some of his essays even made me laugh out loud; the only other thing that made me laugh out loud was *DUH!*

I noticed that Dad's light was still on in his bed-room. I flipped on the kitchen light and opened the refrigerator for some milk. But there wasn't any. I wrote a little note and taped it on the door. After pushing David's dishes out of the way, I sat down at the table with some Ritz crackers and peanut butter. The newspaper was on the chair next to me and I au-tomatically went to the classified ads.

Wanted: Loving Home for Ralph, a cute, lovable, 120-lb. pot-bellied pig. Will eat anything. Loves kids.

For Sale: White Wedding Dress, sequined, strapless. Never worn.

Wanted: Exotic Dancers, friendly, cheer-ful, no experience necessary. Must be fun loving and a people person.

Wanted: Parts and Supplies Distribution Manager for middle-size auto-mobile company. Must have at least ten years' working experi-ence.

I gasped. This was exactly the job Dad had before he'd been laid off. He could go back to work! I couldn't believe my luck; I'd been looking in the want ads for so long I never thought I'd find anything really worthwhile. I began to rip out the ad. It was a local PO Box, which meant that it was nearby. I tore the ad a little by mistake and as I was trying to piece it together, my eye fell on a little black box at the bottom of the page.

"WANTED: A BIG MOUTH. *Your* big mouth. We're looking for kids with something to say. What's your opinion of school? How do you get along with your parents? What do you like about your friends? The *Daily Gazette* is starting a new weekly page called 'Mouth Off' to be conceived, written, and designed by kids age twelve to eighteen. This is a chance to let the world know what you think! If you would like to 'Mouth Off,' please send us an essay on any topic of your choice. The winning essay will appear on the first 'Mouth Off' page."

I quickly tore this ad out, too, and ran to my father's bedroom.

"Dad!" I exclaimed. "You won't believe it! There's an ad for a Parts and Supplies Distribution Manager in the paper. They want someone with lots of experience just like you. It's a PO—"

I stopped at the doorway. Dad was asleep. His reading glasses were on, the lamp was on, and a new book, *How to Turn Your Basement into a Fabulous Rec Room*, was sprawled open on his chest. I tiptoed in, took his glasses off, closed the book, covered him up, and turned the light out.

I put both ads in my bathrobe pocket and went upstairs with Wee-tah.

CHAPTER THIRTEEN

As I turned the corner of my street, I saw my mother's car parked in the driveway. I couldn't believe it! She didn't even mention she was coming home.

Dashing into the house, I dropped my backpack on the kitchen floor.

"Mom!"

She was sitting at the table, writing in a calendar. The phone was tucked under her chin. She blew me a kiss and held up a finger for me to wait.

"Yes. Yes, I understand," she said. "No, it's not a problem. My family understands the travel demands of my job."

Then I noticed the suitcase next to the table. On top of it were some airplane tickets. Mom hung up the phone.

"Evie!"

She threw her arms around me and then pulled me away. "Look at you. You look so . . . so . . . fashionable! What's happened to you?"

I ignored the question. "What are you doing here? You didn't tell anyone you were coming home."

"I know, sweetie," she answered. "And I'm just

home for a bit. I had to get some clothes for the seminar—remember I told you about that?"

"Oh, yeah," I said.

She patted a chair next to her. "Sit down. We can talk for a little while. Dad says you're doing so well at school. That's wonderful."

I nodded. I didn't know where to begin. Or *if* to begin.

"Tell me about your new friends," she said. "What are they like? Have you been to anyone's house?"

"Their names are Lisle and Kristen," I answered. "No, I haven't been to their houses." This was the time to bring up my house problem, but I didn't. Things seemed strange; it was almost as if we didn't know each other well or she was a different person. It was quiet for a few seconds.

"Where's Dad?" I finally asked.

"He ran off to get some things for the deck," she replied.

I looked at her warily. "What do you think about this deck idea?"

She glanced at the clock on the stove. "If he wants to do it, that's great. He's more enthusiastic than he's been in a long time, don't you think?"

"I guess so," I replied. Then I took a deep breath. "But . . . he's not doing other stuff around the house."

She blinked several times and then smiled. "But you should be glad, right? Didn't you always think that I was too neat?"

"You know what I mean, Mom," I contended. "*I'm* not supposed to be the only one cleaning and picking up, am I?"

"No, of course not, Evie. If you feel that way, you should talk to your dad."

I rolled my eyes. She ignored it and stood up. "I have to leave in about fifteen minutes, honey. The traffic to the airport is terrible at this time of day. But I wanted to check up on you before I left."

I felt myself getting angry. "Mom, *you* should talk to Dad. He's not taking care of the house. Tell him what needs to be done."

She took a deep breath and looked at me. "Okay, Eve. You're right. The house is messy and Dad isn't doing as much as I'd like, but he looks happy. Aren't you relieved to see him looking happy?"

I slumped in my seat.

"Okay, then what about David?" I asked. "He's not helping at all."

"I'll call him tonight and talk to him." She picked up the airline tickets and glanced again at the clock. "But what does all of this matter when you're liking school and making friends?"

When I didn't say anything, she came around and gave me a hug. "Evie, I want you to know that I appreciate everything you're doing. Dad's doing great, and so are you. If the house is a little dirtier than usual, that's not so bad, is it?"

Now she was making me feel like Martha Stewart or something.

"I guess not." I picked at some dried ketchup on the table. "How long will you be gone?"

"Just two weeks," she answered, picking up her suitcase.

"Two weeks! Are you kidding? That's such a long time!"

She laughed. "Oh, it'll fly by. By the time I get back, you'll be so busy with your friends you'll barely notice me. And when I get back, I promise to cook your favorite dinners for a week. How's that?"

She picked up her suitcase and opened the back door.

"Wait." I jumped out of my seat. "But you just got here."

"I know, honey, and I'm sorry," she said. "My plane takes off in an hour and a half."

"But, but, Mom . . ." My voice petered out. I didn't have anything else to say. For once in my life.

"I can't wait to meet those new friends of yours, honey."

I followed her outside. She opened the car trunk and put her suitcase inside.

"But Dad's going to be back soon. Can't we take you to the airport?"

She opened the car door and got in. "No, no, no. Why should you two get stuck in traffic? Besides, Dad's too busy."

Starting the car, she motioned for me to come close. I leaned in the window and gave her a hug.

"Bye, sweetie. I'll call when I get to my hotel," she said. "Give David a kiss for me."

Then she backed out of the driveway, beeped the horn, and waved goodbye. I waved back.

I felt six years old and sixty at the same time.

CHAPTER FOURTEEN

It was lunchtime. I had to stop at my locker to put away my books and get my lunch and my math homework for Lisle. Since I was desperately trying to keep her off the topic of the rest of my life, I felt I had to do this even though I hated it. It was better than letting her cheat during a quiz in class.

Kristen and Lisle had left for lunch without me so they could get our favorite table, the one smack in the middle, which gave you the best view. I grabbed my lunch bag and slammed my locker door. Then I turned around and crashed into Seth, who was standing behind me, talking to Lydia at her locker.

"Excuse me," I muttered.

But he ignored me because he was in the middle of telling Lydia a story. I was sort of surprised to see them together. Not that it meant anything, of course, but I just figured that Seth, with his green Mohawk and six earrings, only hung out with kids who looked like him. And Lydia, too, for that matter. As I walked down the hall I heard Lydia burst into a laughing fit and when I looked back, the two of them were doubled over. I wondered what the story was about. I couldn't remember the last time I laughed that hard, even at one of my own jokes. Kristen and Lisle laughed like that sometimes, but it was over stuff like Lydia's stretch pants.

I walked into the lunchroom. It was crowded and noisy, as usual, but there was Kristen, waving her baby wave at me. I sat down next to her, across from Lisle, and opened my lunch bag, which had the same thing in it every day: peanut butter and straw-berry jelly on whole wheat. I told Lisle and Kristen that I had a lot of food allergies and it was dangerous for me to eat any new foods, so my mother—being in the medical field, after all—thought it was best for me to just eat the same food every day. Lisle looked skeptical, of course, but she didn't say anything.

Kristen gave me a sad look. "I can't believe you have to eat the same thing every day. I'd be, 'Oh no, not *again*!'"

Lisle rolled her eyes in agreement as she took a micro-bite out of a Ritz bit. (Lisle took micro-bites out of everything, even a raisin.)

I shrugged my shoulders like I was deeply famil-iar with sacrifice.

"I was in your neighborhood with my mom yes-terday and we were going to stop by," Lisle re-marked casually, "but I wasn't sure of your address." She paused. "What is it again?"

My stomach flip-flopped.

"Nine—" I started to answer but my throat con-stricted. I drank some milk and said the number of the house next door, "Nine seventy-six Glenn. But I wasn't home yesterday." I bit my sandwich and took a risk. "It's probably better if you call first."

Lisle tossed her hair back and said in an icy voice, "Kristen and I practically *live* at each other's house."

Kristen chimed in. "Yeah. Like, Lisle's mom is *soooo* nice. She's like my other mom."

There was a tense silence. My heart was beating fast.

Lisle looked me. "Yeah. Weren't your best friends at your old school like that?"

"Oh, sure," I blurted. "I mean, we, uh . . ."

"Ooh, ooh, there's Zoe," said Kristen in a loud whisper. "Can you believe that hairdo? It looks like road kill!"

I was saved; the lunchtime show had begun. Lisle started to giggle and covered her mouth with her hand. I joined in. We all tried to put on straight faces as Zoe walked by. She gave us a dirty look.

"There's Vampira," muttered Lisle, picking out a chocolate chip from her granola bar to eat separately. "Look! Her nose ring is hanging off one side!"

Kristen almost choked on her fat-free yogurt. I tried not to laugh, remembering how brave Vanessa was to stand up to Mrs. Henry about the "ladylike" noises, but I couldn't help it. Besides, if I didn't, Lisle would wonder why I wasn't joining in.

"Oh, wow," Kristen whispered, recovering. "Look at Brandy, over there, near the window. She dripped some ice cream on her black sweater! Like, on her boob!"

"Which was really tacky-looking to begin with," added Lisle, nibbling half of a Goldfish cracker. "There's Ian." She motioned with her chin. Ian was reading the latest *DUH!* "He actually looks normal in that denim shirt. But he's still too weird; I mean, who else would read *DUH!*?"

I coughed and turned to watch Brady sit down next to Ian. He pointed at something in the magazine. They both laughed.

"Eve, why don't you just take out a telescope," muttered Lisle. "Which one are you staring at, anyway?"

I looked away instantly.

Kristen piped up. "Check it *out.* Taylor's jeans are so long she *tripped* on them." She gasped. "No! Wait!" We all held our breath. "She did it on purpose so that she could grab Donny's arm and walk with him! I can't believe it! He would never like someone like her! E-E-UW! Now she's acting like they're attached at the hip."

Donny was wearing his jacket because under it was his tank top and tank tops weren't allowed at school, even when it was over twenty degrees.

Lisle sighed in disgust and looked directly at Kristen. "He looks dumb in his surfer clothes. Plus, he's conceited."

Kristen was taken by surprise; for a split second she looked at Lisle with contempt. But then it was gone. Forever.

"Yeah," she said quietly. "Really conceited."

Silence.

They both turned to me.

"Right," I said quickly. "Really, *really* conceited."

Okay, so I was mean and awful. I couldn't help it. I'd never realized the joy of talking about everyone at lunch with your friends. It was probably the most wonderful thing of being part of a group. Okay, I felt a little bad because gossip sounded worse spoken out loud—as opposed to just thinking it yourself, hiding behind your *DUH!*—but I also knew that lots of other people in this lunchroom were probably saying mean stuff at this very minute about me and Lisle and Kristen, so it all evens out in the end.

Doesn't it?

I stuck my hand into my pants pocket for some dessert money and felt something, some little pieces of wadded-up paper. I unfolded them in my lap. One was the ad for the Parts Distribution Manager; the other, the ad for the Big Mouth.

I read it over again and then I got a brainstorm, which is not a small thing when you've got the brain that never sleeps; it's more like a tornado with dangerous lightning and howling winds and flying branches. I thought, why not, just why the heck not; we all have to start someplace, don't we?

Even Mark Twain had to start someplace.

Mouth Off: It Feels Good to Be Bad, or How Gossiping Keeps Civilization from Going Kaput.

"Look at that girl over there," your friend whispers to you at lunchtime. "She's bursting out of those pants, her hair looks like she poured Crisco on it, her green eye shadow is up to her forehead, and she's throwing herself at that guy who doesn't even know she's there."

Wasn't that fun to hear? Okay, you don't want to admit it, but it was, right? You don't want to admit it because it was also mean. Nasty. Catty. But it was fun. In fact, the meaner the fun-ner. Why is that? Well, for one thing, *you* weren't the one being whispered about. Of course, that girl—the one who's bursting out of her pants—could go and whisper those exact words to her friend. About you.

Whispering about other people is a very tricky business. Even just listening to other people whisper about other people is tricky business. You might feel bad about it and pretend, well, since I didn't do the actual whispering, I didn't really mean it. Or you can pretend, well, I'm not even sure I heard anyone whispering mean stuff about how Susie looks like a hippo in her new miniskirt. But that's a bunch of baloney. And you know it.

What people love about whispering mean stuff is that they are breaking rules. Which is weird because people also love having rules. They say that they don't, but they do. Otherwise they wouldn't always tell you that you're not supposed to step on the grass or touch anything in a store or slurp your soup or suck up a strand of spaghetti or sit in the teacher's chair when she's gone for a minute or the rest of the gazillions of rules that we have to think about from the moment we wake up until the moment we turn off the light. (That's the last rule: Turn your light off.) In fact if you add up all the rules you hear in one average day it's about forty-five.

So human beings spend tons of time thinking up rules and then try to think up ways to break them. I'm not talking here about big rules like bank robbery. I'm talking about rules like: You must always be polite. So that if someone looks like a stuffed kielbasa in a new tube top you don't tell her that. You tell her that it's nice to see someone who's rebelling against the skinny look. And if someone's hair looks like Crisco, you remark that oil treatments are absolutely necessary for healthy hair. You say this sincerely. Because if everybody walked around telling everyone else that they looked fat and had greasy hair, then everyone's feelings would be hurt and no one could go to school or do their jobs because they'd just be yelling back, "Oh yeah? Well, I never told you this, but you have dandruff and your stomach sticks out of those stirrup pants." And there would probably be crying and screaming and people might even get thrown in jail for just having big mouths. In other words, it would be just like what we read in Mr. Richardson's history class about the people who lived in ancient Rome: Everyone was going so crazy all the time that they didn't even notice when everything around them just went . . . kaput.

But people can get away with breaking the rules, a tiny bit. Instead of actually saying mean stuff about other people out loud they can whisper the mean stuff to their friends. And whoever is being whispered about can always whisper the same stuff to her friends about the first whisperers. It's not so terrible, and it does make school a little more exciting.

So, while I'm not exactly saying that whispering mean stuff helps keep people civilized, I am saying that it's better than being told you look like a stuffed kielbasa to your face.

CHAPTER FIFTEEN

It was several mornings later and I was eating my cereal at the kitchen table. I had taped the ad for Parts Distribution Manager on the refrigerator (next to the "We're out of milk" note) the other night, but it must have fallen off. So I'd found it again in the paper this morning, cut it out, and put it next to the coffeepot. I could hear Dad coming downstairs.

"Hi, Dad," I said.

"Good morning, honey," he replied, going over to the sink. I heard him fill up the teakettle with water and take the coffee out of the refrigerator. Then he came over to the table, pulled out the sports section, and began reading. Maybe he didn't see the ad. I got up and went over to the sink to check. It was gone. I looked around on the floor; maybe it fell. But I didn't see it anywhere.

"Dad," I said. "Did you see that ad for the Parts Distribution Manager?"

He didn't look up from the newspaper.

"Dad?"

"Wow," he muttered. "Fernandez is really in a slump."

"Dad?" I was getting annoyed.

He looked up at me. "Yes, Evie?"

"Did you see that little ad I cut out of the paper for you? About the Parts Distribution Manager?"

He furrowed his brow. Then he shook his head. "No. I don't think so."

I looked on the floor again. I didn't see it. I looked around on the countertop, under the coffeepot, behind the toaster oven, under the microwave, and behind the blender. It was gone. As if it disappeared into thin air.

"Dad, didn't you see a little ad sitting here near the coffeepot?"

He shook his head again.

I went back to the table. "Well, maybe it's in today's want ads."

I stuck a spoonful of cereal in my mouth and sifted through the paper to find the front-page section listing. And then I saw something at the bottom of the front page that made my stomach churn.

A little box that read: "A new place to 'Mouth Off.' On the back page."

I flipped it over and gasped. There it was. My essay. Oh, my God. They didn't even let me know ahead of time. I almost spit out my Frosted Flakes.

"What's the matter?" My dad was looking at me, a worried expression on his face. "Are you okay, Eve?" He strained his neck to see what I was looking at in the newspaper.

"Yeah," I managed to croak, folding the paper up with shaking hands. "I-I-I forgot something upstairs."

Clutching the newspaper, I ran out of the kitchen and up the stairs to my room.

Once inside, I hurled myself onto my bed, held the paper in both hands, closed my eyes, and counted. One, two, three. Eyes open.

It was still there. I read it. I even laughed at a part or two. I looked at the bottom. I had signed myself E. G. O., which stood for Eve, Girl Oddball. I wasn't exactly sure what "ego" meant, but I knew it had something to do with your true self. I figured that I was being my true self in my essay, so it was a good name even though it would have been great to see my real name in print. But I couldn't do that; my essay was written by the old me, not the new. I'd be out of the group in a second.

I folded the paper carefully and put it in my dresser drawer. I felt like I would burst unless I could tell someone about it. But who?

Suddenly Rita nudged her nose in the door and burst into my room, her tail wagging like crazy. She knew that this was one of the best moments of my life. I leaped off my bed and threw my arms around her. I would tell my mom when she made her nightly call.

After a little while I got up, looked in the mirror to make sure I looked okay, then started downstairs. Halfway down, I stopped, because an amazing thought passed through my head: Finally, my "vents," the brain that never sleeps, my inner rantings and ravings that have driven me (and others) crazy, had actually helped me . . . helped me write something that was good enough for the whole world to read.

Is that amazing or what?

When I got downstairs, I could hear my dad moving stuff around in the basement. I was glad. Although he wasn't nearly as good as my mom at just "knowing" when something was up with me, he could occasionally guess. I grabbed my lunch out of the refrigerator and dropped it by mistake as I was opening the back door. As I leaned to pick it up I noticed a small square of newspaper lying on the top of the garbage.

Wanted: Parts and Supplies Distribution Manager.

I stood there blinking at it for a second. Why wouldn't he be interested in it?

I must be missing something.

CHAPTER SIXTEEN

It was later that day and I was in the lobby of Bad-Bods, the smelly health club where my brother worked. Dad had locked himself—and me—out of the house by mistake, so I needed to stop by and get David's house key. I was told by Wonder Woman at the reception desk that David could not be disturbed from his vitally important work, so I was waiting until he had a break. I waved to Dad, who was sitting outside in the car. I'd probably miss Mom's call, because I wasn't home.

Perched on a stainless steel chair, I picked up a magazine from the glass coffee table in front of me. It was called *Mighty Man* and on the cover was a picture of a smiling bodybuilder with shiny, overdeveloped muscles, wearing only a fig leaf. I flipped it open to a letter column.

> Dear Mighty Man:
> I recently purchased an expensive tanning product that promised an even, safe, natural-looking tan. However, halfway through my pectoral display at a recent competition, I began to experience terrible

itching. My skin felt like it was crawling and my whole body turned bright pink. It was very embarrassing. You can imagine how I felt when a doctor there informed me that I'd made medical history with the first case of adult diaper rash all over my body. I sent the tanning product back and have heard nothing from the company. Do you think I should file a lawsuit?

Still Scratching in Des Moines

Dear Still Scratching:

Absolutely! It's important for us body-builders to show product manufacturers that they cannot take advantage of us. Our oversize chests merely give the illusion that our heads are small, but we are not pin-heads. We must fight prejudice and stereo-types! Good luck.

M. M.

I walked back to the reception desk, but Wonder Woman was on the phone with someone who was incredibly witty. In a burst of hysteria, she turned around and pretended I wasn't there.

David has two part-time jobs, one at Eat 'N' Run, a fast-food restaurant for joggers, and the other here at BadBods. Since he studies ex sci, this job was supposed to be a great career opportunity. I know that he hopes to become a personal trainer eventually, which means that among other things, he'll get to carry around clipboards and tell people, okay, that's enough sit-ups, now it's time to do 4,000 leg lifts. That would be a big step up for David because right now his job is to—don't gag—wipe down sweaty exercise equipment after each person uses it. Not surprisingly, he doesn't have much job satisfaction. (I know all about job satisfaction from the want ads.)

Once when I was here, I watched a guy put on a wide leather belt and tighten it so much that he looked like a sausage about to explode. Then he squatted near a dumbbell, put his hands on it, and yanked up—letting out an enormous grunt! Then the other guys in there started grunting when they picked up their weights, too. They all sounded like a bunch of cavemen who needed more fiber in their diets, if you get my meaning.

Anyway, when everyone was done in the weight room, David Belkin, renowned Exercise Equipment Spritzer, was right there on the job, spritzing some blue stuff on the machine and wiping it clean. I found it ironic that David had to do something at work that he never does at home.

David has an amazing talent for never being at home when things go wrong between Mom and Dad. Since it's that way, I figure it must be partly my fault. One day my mother actually told me not to "worry" David with all the trouble Dad was having finding another job. When I asked why not, she said because David had too much on his mind already. Like wiping down StairMasters? I wondered. I was sent to my room for the rest of the evening.

Finally Wonder Woman got off the phone and went to get David. He came around the corner and scowled when he saw me. "Yeah?"

"I need your house key. Dad's locked out."

David grunted at me. It was similar in tone and quality to the dumbbell grunter's. He pulled out his keys and gave them to me. As he turned to go, a familiar voice rang out over the lobby.

"DAAAVVVEEEY?"

It was Ah-wee-sha in all her glory, decked out in black latex shorts, a white thong bottom, and a black sports bra. Alicia taught aerobics here at BadBods, which is how she met David. When he'd wiped some of her sweat off the Butt Buster, it was love at first droplet. She jogged up and gave him a little peck on the cheek. He turned around and went back to work.

I'd never met anyone like Alicia. Her entire life was modeled on fashion magazines; she subscribed to three of them. She thought she lived in the magical girl-magazine land where all the girls are giggling, hugging, blowing bubbles, line dancing, and laughing uproariously together all the time. She had whatever problems they focused on that month ("Water Weight Warning," "Fading Tan Alert") and followed all their trend pronouncements and at-home beauty tips to the T. She even gave David quizzes like "Does he take you seriously?" and "When will he say the L word?"

And even though I know the land of girl magazines is an enormous lie made up by people who just want to sell you a bunch of junk, I'm envious that Alicia has a how-to guide for getting through life.

Alicia turned to me. "Eve, your hair looks terrible. You desperately need a makeover."

"It's nice to see you, too, Alicia," I replied.

She sighed deeply; my sarcasm wasn't going to win me any friends and certainly not any dream hunks. Lifting a leg high on the wall, she adjusted the black headband around her forehead and took a sip of SportsDrink. "If you want, I can help you with your hair tomorrow. That is, if you can manage to act mature for a half hour."

"I don't think I can," I said.

My dad walked inside. "Hi, Alicia. Hey, Eve, I just noticed a plumbing supply place across the street, so I'm going to run there for a minute. I've been wanting to get an estimate on retiling the upstairs bathroom." He stopped. "Oh, I almost forgot. Thanks so much, Alicia, for that great banana bread. It was terrific."

"What banana bread?" I asked.

"Alicia baked some and brought it over this morning," Dad said on his way out the door. "It was so good that David and I ate it in about ten minutes."

Alicia undoubtedly made the banana bread after the other night when she'd had the bad luck to arrive at our house just in time to taste the famous killer chili made with canned tomatoes, kidney beans, hamburger, and Parmesan cheese. Except that we didn't have any kidney beans so my dad used a can of baked beans and he forgot about the hamburger.

Alicia smiled radiantly. "Thanks, Mr. B. I love to cook."

I snorted. My dad gave me a dirty look.

"Yep, that bread was delish, Alicia." He chuckled.

Alicia tossed her head back and twittered. I thought I might puke.

But what else is new?

CHAPTER SEVENTEEN

"Well, people, it's that time again," announced Mrs. Henry. "Put your books under your desk."

You could hear the *uh-ohs* echoing around the room. A famous Mrs. Henry pop quiz. I glanced over at Lisle; she sat in the next row over and a few seats up. She was watching me steadily. I nodded once and looked away.

"Mrs. Henry?" Donny was waving his hand. "I've been *mucho* sick for the last three days."

"But now you're here, *sí*?" Mrs. Henry asked. "Unless, of course, someone engineered a poor unfortunate clone from a person who wears a wet suit in February."

"But my body is stressed out to the max," protested Donny. "I'm not getting enough vitamin D in this climate. I'm *totally* not ready for this quiz."

Kristen looked concerned. Lydia popped a caramel into her mouth, then gave one to Brady. Lisle was angling her desk around.

Mrs. Henry looked pained. "Oh, wait. Let me change into my bikini to remind you of home."

Even Vanessa cracked a smile on that one. Donny gave up and put his head on his desk; his long blond hair hung wistfully over the side. Mrs. Henry started down the aisle with a stack of papers and handed me one.

It was pretty easy; I was done in no time. Lisle was squirming around in her seat. I started to relax because she was too far away to see my test, when suddenly a pencil came flying through the air and landed at my feet. Lisle raised her hand and asked Mrs. Henry if she could pick up her pencil. Mrs. Henry nodded at her, then barked, "Five more minutes, everybody."

Lydia groaned. Brady was screwing up his face like he was in the men's weight room at BadBods. Donny was asleep on his desk, sapped of his strength by his vitamin D deficiency. And Lisle got up to get her pencil.

She walked toward me, pointing at my quiz. She crouched down to get her pencil, and brushed my test to the floor so she could get a longer look. I started to reach for it. But then I heard whispering noises coming from Kristen, who was trying to get Lisle's attention. Lisle ignored her. Kristen was upset and her whispering got louder.

"Kristen, are you having a problem?" asked Mrs. Henry.

"No," answered Kristen.

"But you were turning around in your seat and whispering," said Mrs. Henry. "I think you were looking at Lisle's paper."

"What?" Kristen looked like she'd been slapped. "I wasn't looking at Lisle's paper."

"Then what were you doing?"

Kristen didn't answer because she couldn't say, I was trying to get Lisle to cheat off *me* instead of Eve. Her chin started trembling. "I wasn't looking at her paper."

Mrs. Henry lowered her voice ominously. "I'd like you to go to Mrs. Fletcher's office *now*, Kristen." She looked gravely down at her desk. "And I have to add that I am very disappointed that someone like you would stoop to this."

By this time Lisle was back in her seat, doodling hearts, cool as a cucumber. I'd picked up my quiz and was back in my seat. With shaking hands, I smoothed out my paper.

Was Lisle really going to let Kristen take the blame for her? That's a pretty big price even for the primary Lisle-worshiper.

Kristen packed up her books. When she got to the door she looked at Lisle, who completely ignored her. When she looked at me, I had to look away.

I felt terrible.

CHAPTER EIGHTEEN

I left Lisle in the girls' bathroom and hurried to English class. I wanted to be in the room when everyone else came in, so I could eavesdrop on any conversations about the new Mouth Off page in the paper. But as I sat there listening to Ian telling Vanessa about some bacteria he'd been growing on a hunk of provolone cheese that his sister had used in some fondue for her boyfriend's parents' party, and Seth explaining to Brady that the guy who used to dye his Mohawk lime green had left town and the new guy he went to just had *forest* green, which he didn't like, and Lydia telling Donny that wearing a wet suit in a sauna makes you drop five pounds of water weight immediately, I was losing hope that anyone had even seen my essay. I was very tempted to ask someone—like Lydia or Ian—if they had seen it (something along the lines of, "Hey, did you see that new kids' page in the paper? Did you read that essay on gossiping? Wasn't it fabulous?"). But I didn't. Since I've barely talked to any of them since I'd started school, they'd think it was pretty strange.

Kristen came in by herself and sat down without talking to me.

"Hi, Kristen," I said, cheerily. "How's it going?"

She didn't answer. She obviously blamed *me* for what happened, not Lisle.

Lisle walked in and sat down. Kristen turned to her. "We're still going to the mall today after school, right?"

It was obvious that I wasn't included.

Lisle tossed her hair back and shrugged her shoulders.

Ms. Harley clapped her hands together for attention and then started talking about journalism. I tuned her out as I watched Kristen scribble a note to Lisle, who barely responded. Whenever Lisle caught my eye she rolled her eyes in Kristen's direction. I focused on Ms. Harley so I wouldn't have to be meaner to Kristen.

"For the next writing assignment I would like you to interview someone," Ms. Harley was saying. "Pretend that you're a reporter and find out all you can about that person's likes, dislikes, childhood, family, hopes for the future, thoughts on the world in the year 2025. What makes the person who he or she is?"

Out of the corner of my eye, I could see Kristen was agitated. She was motioning to Lisle, who had tilted her chin up and looked away. Kristen was close to panicking; I couldn't watch.

Now Ms. Harley was passing papers out. "I've copied some famous interviews that I want you to read and analyze. Ask yourselves: What makes them good? What kinds of questions do the interviewers ask? How do they phrase their questions so they get more than a yes or no answer?"

Now Kristen was raising her hand urgently, practically falling out of her seat. "Ms. Harley? Ms. Harley?"

Ms. Harley held up a finger for Kristen to wait a moment. Lisle gave a bored sigh; she was doodling hearts in her notebook. We both knew what Kristen wanted to ask.

"And I'd like you to start thinking about who would make an interesting subject to interview. Questions? Kristen."

"Can we pick anyone we want? Someone in the class?"

Ms. Harley smiled. "You read my mind, Kristen. That's exactly what the assignment is—pick someone in the class to interview, then you switch."

"Lisle," Kristen whispered loudly. "Lisle. You and me? Okay? Lisle!"

Lisle was digging around in her backpack, ignoring her. I tried to melt into my seat.

The class was noisy; everyone was talking to one another.

Ms. Harley clapped her hands. "I greatly encourage you to pick someone whom you don't know that well, someone who seems really different than you. I promise it will make the assignment more interesting."

Lisle looked up, completely ignoring Kristen, and said evenly, "Eve. You and me. Okay?"

I didn't know what to say. I looked at Kristen;

she was on the verge of tears. I looked at Lisle; she was smiling slyly. Part of me wanted to tell Kristen that I didn't want this and that Lisle could go stick her head in a bucket, but another part of me wanted to say, "Ha ha ha ha ha, she likes me better." I felt awful about that part, but it was still there, anyway.

The bell rang and Kristen bolted out of the room.

Lisle and I walked together out of class, toward our lockers. The hallway was quiet; Lisle's chunky black ankle boots made little taps on the floor.

"Do you know what happened when Kristen was sent to Mrs. Fletcher's office?" I asked.

Lisle gave me a surprised look and tossed her hair back. "How would I know what happened? *I've* never been sent there."

"But it wasn't Kristen's fault." This was risky, but I decided to go with it.

Lisle opened her locker and reached up for some books on the top shelf. "It *was* her fault for whispering so loud," she said irritably. "She totally freaks out if she thinks I like someone else better than her for one second. She's incredibly immature."

I didn't know what to say. As much as I felt flattered, I didn't want the responsibility of being liked better than Kristen.

Lisle slammed her locker and put her arm around my shoulders.

"So. When do I finally get invited over to your house?" she said in her fake friendly voice. "I'm dying to see your room."

I busied myself with my coat and books. "I'll have to check with everyone's schedule to see who's going to be home."

We walked out of school and down the wide steps toward the school buses. When my mom gets home, I thought, and things get back to normal, then, maybe she could come over. But no way right now. I had to keep putting her off.

"Well, how about if you come over this weekend? For dinner or a sleepover!" said Lisle, looking at me.

I shook my head. "I can't—"

But then I heard something that made my heart start to pound.

My name. Called out.

In my father's voice.

"Eve! Evie!"

"Someone's calling you," Lisle said, looking around.

"Eve! Over here!"

And then I saw him, parked behind the buses, waving his arms at me. What was he doing here? Oh, God, I thought as I ran over, this is it, the end of it all; he's going to wreck everything for me. . . .

Lisle was right on my heels.

"Dad!" I shouted. "What is it? Is something wrong?" I pulled him around and back a little. Lisle stayed on my tail.

He shook his head. "No, no. Calm down. Everything's fine."

I could see that everything was fine, but I pretended otherwise so I could ignore her for a second longer. It gave me a chance to quickly assess Dad's appearance: blue jeans, parka, hiking boots, hair combed back, face shaven. It was okay.

Dad was talking. "So, I was just running over to HomePro for some duct tape and realized that your school was right on the way. I figured that I might as well stop and pick you up and we could go together."

"Oh." Pause. "Great."

I tried to think of something else to say, some other reason for not acknowledging Lisle yet, but I didn't want Dad to keep talking, either. Lord only knew what might come out of his mouth. He took a step backward and whistled. "Wow, Eve. Don't you look nice. Isn't that the skirt that Grandma gave you that you said looked like wallpaper?"

Lisle cleared her throat behind me.

"Who's behind you, Eve?" Dad poked his head around. "One of your new friends?"

"Oh! I forgot! Dad, this is Lisle."

"Hmm," he said thoughtfully. "Interesting name. Rhymes with 'diesel.'"

Lisle ignored that and chirped, "Hi, Mr. Belkin. I was just trying to talk Eve into coming over this weekend."

They were face-to-face. Talking to each other! I had to make this scene brief; it had disaster written all over it.

Dad turned to me excitedly. "That sounds great, Eve! Sure, you could go to Lisle's house, that would be fine."

"How about for dinner? And a sleepover?" Lisle was actually perky.

"Um, um." I couldn't think fast enough. I glared at my dad, willing him to keep his mouth shut. I didn't want to sleep over there, it would only make it harder for me to avoid having her over. Besides, sleep deprived, I could break down and tell her anything, which happens a lot on *The Twilight Zone*. "I can't sleep over," I said. "But I guess dinner would be okay."

I saw my dad open his mouth and shook my head. Please, just be quiet, don't say anything, like Eve hasn't gone to any friends' houses for ages, or Eve's never been invited to a sleepover, or . . .

"Sure! You could slee—" he blurted.

I mouthed the words to him, "No, no, no."

He scrunched up his face. "What?"

Lisle was watched us both intently. I looked around for help and saw the school buses.

"Lisle," I said excitedly. "It looks like your bus is almost ready to leave." I could see my father opening his mouth to offer Lisle a ride home. "Dad? One of the back tires looks like it needs air, doesn't it?"

I felt like I was juggling flaming torches. "Come on," I took Lisle's arm. "I'll walk you to the bus. What time is good for Saturday?"

She glanced back at my dad, who was kicking the back tire. I was speed walking to the buses. Lisle looked puzzled. "Um, how about around five?"

"Great," I said. "I'll see you then. Bye!"

Lisle called out, "Bye, Mr. Belkin!"

He waved. I walked back to him and took a deep sigh of relief.

"Which tire looked flat?" he asked.

"No tire, Dad, I just didn't want to sleep over at her house."

"Why? She seemed perfectly nice," he said, opening the car door for me.

"She's not," I replied.

"I can't believe a girl like that isn't nice," he remarked, starting up the car. "You're just saying that because she looks neat and nicely dressed."

"Well, *you're* just saying she's nice because she looks neat and nicely dressed," I pointed out perceptively. Too perceptively, I guess, because he gave me a puzzled look.

I sighed. Some things never change.

Mouth Off: You Are
What You Wear. Not.

If Freddy Krueger showed up at your door wearing penny loafers, Levi's Dockers, and a polo shirt, would your parents let you go out with him? If they're like mine, they'd give him twenty dollars, the car keys, and ask if he had a prom date yet.

Parents get stupid when kids look neat. Why is that? Even if you say to them, "Who? That guy? He's totally obnoxious, no one can stand him, and he gets in trouble constantly at school," you've lost your case if his shirt is tucked in. If his pants have creases, you might as well be speaking in foreign tongues. Because parents think neatness is all. They attribute positive characteristics to people who look neat. Looking neat automatically means someone is nice. A belt means someone is a good student. Clean, combed hair equals homework done right after school. Shiny, tied shoes are the same as doing the dinner dishes without being asked.

What is this mass insanity that afflicts parents? I'll tell you what it is, it's prejudice. The same kind of prejudice that your parents tell you not to practice. Parents are neat-bigots. They would, in test after test, pick a neatly dressed person to be your friend regardless of what that person might be like.

In fact, their hypocrisy is amazing. If you told them that you desperately wanted a pair of mauve satin gym shorts and a matching snakeskin bomber jacket they would lecture you about how bad it is to care about clothes so much, how it really doesn't matter how you look because it's what's *inside* that counts, and no one is going to like you better if you are wearing something cool or not and if they do then they aren't worth having as friends. So instead you dig out your Mom's old tie-dye overalls, find an old bowling shirt of your brother's, and borrow your dad's cowboy hat and *then* they tell you that you can't be serious about wanting to go out of the house looking like that. If you give them the "it's-what's-inside-that-counts" schtick and ask them why, since "clothes aren't important," do they care how you look when you go out, they'll just warn you about "an attitude problem" (which we know—and they know—really means you've won).

And the real clincher is that these neat kids are no dummies. They aren't simply wearing neat clothes because they *want* to. Noooo! They know what goes with neatness. With neatness goes honor, trust, responsibility, decency, manners, and all those other words parents are always flapping about their kids "earning." And who earns it faster? A guy with dreadlocks who twists his ankle in his grunge pants? Or a cheerful psychopath in a Ralph Lauren blazer with nicely trimmed hair? I don't have to spell it out for you.

Does Freddy walk around in some black getup with skeleton heads on it? Not always. The nice kid down the street wears stuff like that; Freddy could be in chinos.

The only solution is for sloppy kids of the world to unite. We must prove to our parents that although we might have our size 18 sweatshirts on inside out and backward, it doesn't mean we're stupid, lazy, or inconsiderate. Show them that you can look however you want and still be an upstanding kid. Become an example. Dry the dinner dishes with the part of your T-shirt that comes down to your knees. Ace that spelling test even though your bangs are in your eyes. Zip through that homework with a spare pencil in case you lose one in your shirtsleeve.

Talk to your parents gently about judging books by their covers and that sort of stuff. In time they'll understand. And if all else fails, rent *Nightmare on Elm Street*.

CHAPTER NINETEEN

It was Saturday morning and I slept late, exhausted from my double life, which sounded mysterious and romantic but was just draining. I finally talked to my mom last night and told her about the Mouth Off essays. She screamed with joy. She said she couldn't wait to read them. I felt really great until the phone rang again. I thought it might be Mom again but it was Lisle, re-inviting me for dinner and a sleepover. The famous brain was caught unawares and I couldn't come up with any excuse. So I was going there for dinner tonight. I tried not to dwell on it.

And that was pretty easy to do because it was the weekend and the Belkin household *sans* mother was in top form. First thing Saturday morning, Dad dropped his new hammer on his toe. You may be thinking: Ah, good, at least he's working, right? Not exactly. It happened when he was *washing*—yes, you read that correctly—*washing* the new hammer to get the price tag off it. What happened was that the hammer slipped out of Dad's hands and landed on his big toe. Dad limped into the den to keep his foot raised on the sofa.

Then David woke up and made his "vita-drink," which consists of ingredients that you don't want me to list, but he didn't tighten the blender top and when he turned it on, it spurted, like a waterspout, all over the kitchen. Then Rita licked some of the vita-drink that was lying near her bowl and threw up all over the dining room carpeting. So now we had the original vita-drink accident in the kitchen and the canine-regurgitated vita-drink in the dining room. I felt sort of queasy and went into the bathroom, planning to douse my face with cold water except that the sink had been taken out.

The house was under assault. In the refrigerator and bathroom, bacterial life flowered. Giant hairballs blew across the wooden floors like tumbleweeds in the desert, a leaning tower of aluminum TV-dinner trays swayed on the coffee table in the den, and on every conceivable surface there was a dirty glass, bowl, or plate covered with a thin, greasy film.

I'd stopped asking my father about all the stuff that wasn't getting done. He obviously didn't consider it as important as his "projects." I'd felt like a nag and resented it, especially since it was *his* fault I was nagging him. So now I was trying to do my share of cleaning while trying to ignore the state of the rest of the house, the way Dad and David seemed to do effortlessly. But it was hard. Very hard. And it was even harder to be civil to my dad: "patience" and "understanding" were out the window.

Anyway, to proceed with the morning's events:

After the vita-drink accident, I went outside to get the morning paper. I made it quick in case Lisle was around somewhere. On top of my other problems, paranoia was adding a whole new dimension.

I flipped to the letters page, looking for that one person who, by accident, spilled juice on the paper and happened to read my Freddy Krueger essay and then wrote in to say it was terrible. But of course, there was nothing.

I was now convinced that no one, not one, single, solitary person on the face of the earth had read my essay. What would Mark Twain have done in this situation? He would have written a wonderfully satiric essay on the boundless stupidity of his fellow man. But he probably had more energy than me because he had a wife who kept his house neat and clean and cooked him food other than killer chili.

I passed by David leaning against a tree with his leg up, doing warm-up exercises in his new fluorescent green unitard running outfit that looked like something Barbie's Ken would wear in his Power Gym.

As I watched him I thought, Come on, he couldn't really go running and leave that disgusting mess all over the kitchen.

Could he?

"What are you doing?" I asked him.

"What does it look like, brainiac? I'm going for my run," he answered, putting one foot forward and bending over it. His unitard went riding up into his "gluteals," the workout word for butt.

"But what about the kitchen?"

"Alicia's in there," he yelled, running down the street.

"So?" I yelled back. He was gone. I walked in the front door, almost colliding with Alicia, who was carrying a small flowered tray with a plate of toast and some scrambled eggs on it.

"What are you doing here?" I asked.

"I came over to bring some clean sheets and towels for David," she answered, taking tiny steps backward down the hall. "And when I saw your poor dad lying on the couch with his sore toe, I offered to fix him breakfast."

With that she turned and walked into the den to serve my father. A bit confused, I continued into the kitchen, realizing only then that Alicia had been wearing an . . . apron. A white, frilly one that she probably got out of Victoria's Secret.

When I reached the kitchen I now saw why Alicia had on her adorable apron: because she'd cleaned up David's drink mess. So let's recap, here, shall we? Alicia's boyfriend spilled his gross, smelly drink all over the kitchen and she hopped out of bed on a Saturday morning, dashed over, and cleaned it all up. Just like that. And, while she was here cleaning up the mess (which included her boyfriend's dog's throw-up), Alicia noticed that her boyfriend's poor father was hurt, neglected, and starving, so she decided that she was going to cook *and* serve him some breakfast . . . on a tray.

This was too much. Since I was in a bewildered

stupor, I didn't notice that someone had come back into the kitchen. But now I became aware of running water and movements near the stove. I sat up and focused. It was Alicia mopping the kitchen floor.

"Alicia, what are you doing?"

She turned to me. "What's it look like I'm doing? I'm mopping the floor."

"I know that." I took a deep breath. "But, *why*?"

"Because it's *dirty*," she said, like I was the biggest imbecile in the universe.

"But why are *you* doing it?"

"Because I can't stand dirty floors," she answered.

"And you cleaned up the vita-puke, too, right?"

She stopped to carry a chair into the hall so she could mop under it. "Yeah. Who else would have done it? The tooth fairy? Certainly not *you*."

"But why?" I raised my voice a notch. "Why did *you* clean it up? It was David's mess."

She gave an exasperated sigh, not looking up from the floor. "He's really busy. He doesn't have time."

Even though what she was saying made sense in one way, in another way it made no sense at all. Everything was wrong. What if I had a boyfriend and he came over and did the stuff that Alicia did? What would we call him? A butler? A wimp? Stupid?

"Hey, Alicia," came a shout from the den. "Those eggs were terrific! How come guys never know how to make scrambled eggs like that?"

Um, let's see. Because the gene for making scrambled eggs is carried in the X chromosome?

"How about a couple more?" my dad called.

Alicia beamed. "Sure!" She practically tripped over her bucket of water in a hurry to get to the refrigerator.

I started to read the want ads.

"Don't you ever make breakfast for your dad?" Alicia asked as she cracked each egg with one hand and flung the shells in a perfect arc into the garbage can.

"Um, no, I mean, yeah," I answered. "I fix him some cereal when I'm having some."

Alicia snorted. "I didn't mean cereal. Anybody can do *that*." She picked up the salt and pepper shakers with a flourish and suddenly shouted, "Mr. Belkin? How about a cheese omelet?"

"My favorite!" my father yelled back.

Now she's just showing off, I thought, watching her open the refrigerator. I realized (with a thrill) that she wouldn't find any cheese in there, except the blue-crusted variety. But suddenly she was wielding a new package of cheddar cheese. Ripping it open, she grabbed a shredder, and started shredding the cheese from high up, over the pan. It was beginning to smell wonderful.

"Smells wonderful, Alicia, honey," yelled my dad.

"Alicia, where did you get that cheese?" I asked. "I didn't think we had any."

"You didn't. I brought it over, with the clean towels," she answered, dashing over to the toaster and popping two slices of bread in.

"But why?"

107

"Because David loves cheddar cheese!" she replied, flipping the omelet in the air, a feat I had only seen performed by the lady on *Hook 'im with Cookin'*.

"But why?"

There must have been a note of despair in my voice because finally she turned to me and spoke slowly and deliberately. "Because I *like* to cook, I *like* taking care of him; it makes me feel needed. He appreciates it. Your dad appreciates it." She paused. "There. Is that clear enough for you?"

Then she scooped the omelet out of the pan and arranged it perfectly between the two pieces of whole wheat toast. She placed the plate on the tray and started out of the kitchen.

No, I thought to myself as she walked past me and I tried to ignore the growling in my stomach. It is not clear. Not in the slightest.

Mouth Off: How to Flip an Omelet, Make a Peanut Butter Sandwich, Braid Hair, and 1,001 Other Things That Girls Are Supposed to Know.

Sure, you may think: What's so great about flipping an omelet? I don't care about omelets; I don't even like them. And if I did, I wouldn't care if it was flipped or not. Or if it *was* flipped, I wouldn't care if it was perfectly flipped or some of it got smushed or ended up on the wrong side. It wouldn't matter.

So the general opinion is that flipping an omelet is not a skill that you desperately need to get through life. Right? Right. Except if you're a girl. Now, before you get all worked up about how girls are treated exactly like boys these days, just hear me out. No, girls don't *have* to know how to flip an omelet. But even though people say that it's not important for a girl to know stuff like that, they sort of expect it. It's one of those expectations that people don't even think about because it's taken for granted.

I'll give you an example: Let's say a boy and a girl play soccer together and come back for a peanut butter sandwich. If the girl said, "I have no idea how to make a peanut butter sandwich," the boy would probably be surprised and the girl would probably feel embarrassed. However, if the boy said that, the girl wouldn't be that surprised and might even think it was cute—a typical boy. He might even think it's not manly to know how to make a peanut butter sandwich. It's like that for flipping an omelet, too.

This principle can be applied to lots of things that girls aren't "required" to know these days but when they see that other girls do know how to do those things, they get worried. Are they okay? Are they normal girls? Should I know how to do that stuff? Why haven't I learned? And, who is supposed to teach me?

Let's take hair braiding, as another example. Sure, you can live your life quite comfortably without knowing how to braid your hair and feel like you are a perfectly adequate person. But then one day you go over to your friend's house and you see that everyone knows how to braid hair. And not just how to braid hair but how to put it in two braids and twist it in two loops around your ears so you look like you're ready to yodel; or make those teeny-weeny strands of occasional braids with beads in them that seem incredibly tedious; or a French braid that rises out of the chaos of your head without even so much as a rubber band. Sure, you might beat your father at chess, but the part in your hair looks like the Grand Canyon.

So the next time you see someone doing something that you can't do but feel you can't confess to them, I say speak up! Maybe the way *you* do things isn't the same way *they* do things, but it suits you just fine. When that boy wonders why you can't make a peanut butter sandwich, ask him why he can't, either. When that girl wonders why your braid is lopsided and falling out, tell her that you like the disheveled look, and when you see someone flipping an omelet, tell them that you like yours scrambled.

CHAPTER TWENTY

I was at the BuyMart, maneuvering my hair in front of my face to hide my identity while I secretly read *Girl Talk*. I even grabbed a copy of *Forbes* (the magazine next to *Girl Talk*) so I could quickly flash it over the other magazine if necessary. I was scanning the page on "New Products That Spell Fun!" so if the conversation at Lisle's drifted into the direction of the latest trends, I'd be prepared.

For example, I could tell her about "BelliButtons," to dress up your belly button! Get the cutest selections for that special sexy spot. In love? You need the Heart Belli. Love animals? Wear the adorable Kitty Belli. Want to express yourself? An Initial Belli. No matter what kind of mood you're in, there's a Belli to match it. So whether you have an "outty" or an "inny," show it off with Bellies!

And in case you haven't found something else to feel worried about there's "Bare of Hair" facial-hair remover, because you're never too young to have unwanted facial hair. Bare of Hair removes all traces of ugly, embarrassing facial hair. Your skin will be clear, smooth, and baby-fresh soft. Bare of Hair can be used safely on your chin, cheek, nose, or any place you never imagined hair could grow but once you thought about it you were horrified that you might have it. Only $19.95 for a month's supply. Save! Buy a six-month supply for only $110.00!

Why is it okay for men to look like gorillas but women have to undergo medieval torture to get rid of unwanted hair? I imagined putting on my puppy dog BelliButton after I smeared a nice thick slab of smelly white Bare of Hair over my upper lip.

I laughed out loud.

"Try this month's *DUH!*" said a voice way too close to me. "It's *supposed* to be funny."

I shrieked and jumped about ten feet, hurling *Girl Talk* high into the air. Ian was standing behind me, holding the latest issue of *DUH!*

"What are you doing here?" I asked stupidly, smoothing my hair back behind my ears.

"The same thing as you are," he answered. "Trying to read a magazine all the way through without having to buy it. But I hadn't thought of trying to hide behind my hair."

With poise and grace I leaned over to put the *Forbes* magazine in its place, making a deep sigh like I was weary from reading it. I cleared my throat.

"Yes, I always flip through a variety of magazines. It broadens my horizons, gives me a good view of what's happening in the world," I said without laughing. Ian, however, couldn't listen without laughing.

"I'm very impressed that you could say that with

a straight face," he said. "Have you ever thought about doing stand-up comedy?"

"As a matter of fact, I do some great impersonations," I replied. "For my dog."

"And," he asked, "does she bark?"

I shook my head. "She wags."

He nodded. "So how's Princess Lisle and her entourage?"

I didn't know what to say. I hadn't even spoken to Ian since I'd started school, so I wanted to say, "I'm just hanging around with her to help my parents, yet I'm actually a brilliant writer whose essays have been in the newspaper, but I must remain anonymous for the sake of . . . myself." By now I was in too deep with Lisle. I couldn't explain my plan to him, and besides, then he would just think I was a big phony, which I was, of course.

I shrugged my shoulders. "She's okay. What did you think of this month's *DUH!*'s 'Favorite Flubs?'"

Ian ignored my attempt to change the subject and peered at me through his glasses. "You don't seem like those girls. You seem like . . ."

"What?" I waited, holding my breath. Brilliant? Witty? A mindless follower?

He didn't say any more, and I just looked down and pretended to scrape something off my jeans.

"But at least you were laughing at that stupid *Girl Talk.* That's a good sign. Hey, where did you throw it, anyway?" he asked, looking around.

Surveying the area, I finally saw it lying on top

of a giant Pepto-Bismol display. I nudged Ian and pointed.

"Wow, now, there's brilliant marketing," he whispered. "A complimentary bottle of Pepto-Bismol with every *Girl Talk* magazine."

We walked over to get it. "Hey," he exclaimed, turning to me. "I just thought of something. Do you want to interview each other for school?"

"Uh . . . um." Yes! I wanted to yell. But could I get out of it with Lisle? Tell her that I'm suffering from hair-gel seepage into my brain? Or that my scrunchee was too tight and pulled a head muscle?

"I . . . can't," I finally said, looking down. We both knew why.

"That's okay, I'll just ask old Lyd. The problem with her is that we've been friends since kindergarten, so we know pretty much everything about each other."

Hearing that made me envious: How great to know someone so well and for such a long time that you know everything about them; I couldn't imagine what that felt like. The only people who knew me that well *had* to because they were related to me.

Ian looked at his watch. "Well, I've got to get going. I need to find . . ." He looked up at the ceiling. "The home improvement aisle."

I pointed a few rows away. "Over there. Number six." I knew every home improvement aisle number in town.

"Now, what do I need to get?" Ian furrowed his brow. "Oh yeah. Some brushes and two gallons of polyurethane for my mom. She's almost done with the hardwood floors she's put down in the dining room, but *then* she starts her next project of turning the attic into a guest bedroom. Luckily, my dad's the neat one—otherwise we'd all be living in a construction site."

He waved as he walked away. "See you Monday."

I waved back.

Life was becoming too complicated.

CHAPTER TWENTY-ONE

My dad and I were in the car on our way to Lisle's house. I decided that I had to talk to him. When we reached the end of our block, I took a deep breath.

"Dad, I heard you on the phone a few days ago."

"What? When? What's this guy doing ahead of me?"

"Around dinnertime the other night. Someone from your old job. I was opening the fruit cocktail for dessert, so I couldn't help overhearing."

"Yeah, that jerk Brayhauser called, 'to see how I was holding up.' Patronizing creep."

Uh-oh. "Yeah, that guy. Um . . ."

"Great! Just pull out right in front of me, moron."

"Um . . . it sounded like that jerk Brayhauser was talking about a job."

"Wonderful! Pull out in front of me, *then* go five miles an hour."

"Did he? Brayhauser? Say something about a job?" I knew I was on dangerous ground here but I had a plan. Sort of.

Long pause. "Yeah, he did."

"Your old job?"

"No. Something in the quality control department."

116

"Oh! That sounds interesting!" I was positive. Supportive. Nauseating.

Snort.

"Are they going to offer it to you?"

Another snort.

"Don't you want to get it?" The snorts were confusing me.

"Not if I have to jump through hoops, I don't."

Pause. "What does 'jump through hoops' mean?"

"It means having to perform like an animal in the circus."

Pause. "I don't get what you mean."

"It means having to compete with other people for the position. It means having to pass whatever kind of test they've devised."

"Oh." I hadn't thought of that.

"I'm not interested."

Pause. "Why not? *You* could pass the test."

Silence.

"Right, Dad?" How hard could it be?

"I'm not going back there. Eighteen years of my life didn't count for anything. In the end, I was just dispensed with. I'm through being a paper pusher. That kind of work is just not important to me anymore."

"Oh."

"Wow, your new friend lives in a fancy neighborhood. Here's Wellington Drive. What's the address again?"

"Six hundred."

"Okay, it should be coming up."

"Then what kind of work is important, Dad?" This was an opening—

"Well, I think what I'm doing at home is important. Don't you?"

"Um, I guess so. But what about—"

He cut me off. "I'm renovating the bathroom, the basement, the kitchen. It's going to increase the value of our house—"

I cut him off. "But what about work around the house? Housework? Like cooking and cleaning and stuff like that. Don't you think that's important? Oh, forget it. Mom is coming home in two days anyway."

"Wait a minute, Eve." His voice had an edge. "Haven't we *all* been pitching in to keep things going while Mom's been away?"

"Well, yeah, I guess so." I was sorry I'd brought it up.

"Everyone does things his own way, Eve. Mom is more organized than me, I'll admit that. But she doesn't think of long-term projects."

"The house is dirty, Dad. There's no food in the refrigerator. No one is remembering to take the garbage out or clean the bathrooms or—"

"You're exaggerating. Okay, maybe the house is messy, but it's not dirty. At least, *I* don't think it's dirty. And there *is* food in the refrigerator. Alicia just whipped up a delicious omelet for me this morning. So I missed garbage day, big deal. And you did some laundry the other day. I thought that was okay with you."

"Here's six hundred Wellington Drive. It *was* okay with me. That's not really what I meant—"

"And that's another thing. We moved to a new town and you've made some nice friends already, more than you've ever had. This has been a great success for you. Right? And we did it without Mom. You should be proud of yourself."

Deep sigh.

"And now you're going to dinner at your new friend's house for the first time. Here we are." He smiled and tickled me in the side. "Have fun, you little worrywart. I'll see you later."

I got out of the car and slammed the door hard.

CHAPTER TWENTY-TWO

The gigantic front door squeaked as it opened slowly. I was a little nervous about being here; if I were in a movie this would be the part when the scary violins start playing. A blonde head appeared around the door.

"I'm Mrs. Penfield. You must be Eve."

She opened the door wide and swung her arm in a large arc, like one of those ladies on *The Price Is Right* displaying her runner's-up prize of a year's supply of Del Monte lima beans. I stepped inside.

"Welcome to our home," she said, shutting the door firmly behind me.

"Thank you," I muttered. I looked at Lisle's mother. I should say I looked *up* at Lisle's mother because she was very tall. Her hair was so light blonde it looked almost white. It was in one of those TV-anchor type of styles: no nonsense, yet soft around the edges. A hairstyle that's easily recognizable as "a mother's hairdo."

My mom usually wears her long hair in a ponytail. When she leaves her hair long you can see the gray streaks in it. I can't decide if the gray looks good, like she doesn't care, or bad, like she doesn't care. It's not the easiest mother hairdo to decipher.

Now Mrs. Penfield held her hand out to me. I shook it tentatively. Mrs. Penfield's hand was cool and dry and tinkling with jewelry. She wore a matching pants and sweater outfit in one of those noncolors—ivory, taupe, beige—that also matched the colors of the furniture and carpeting. Everything about her was perfect. Everything in her home was perfect. She was her home.

"Lisle will be down in a jiffy."

I followed her into the white, gleaming kitchen. She tied on a pink flowered apron and brandished some matching oven mitts. I heard footsteps and Lisle walked into the room. She smiled at me and tossed her hair. I gazed at Lisle and her mother. They were so alike, not in the way they looked necessarily, but in the way they . . . were. I realized that life was a lot easier if you wanted to be just like your mother. *I* loved my mother, but I wanted to be different.

I heard a door slam and a man walked into the kitchen.

"Hi, sweetheart!" called Mrs. Penfield, waving an oven mitt. "It's baked ham with pineapple chunks, your favorite!"

"Hi, Dad," said Lisle. "This is my friend Eve. She's the one I've told you about who just moved here a couple of months ago."

He put his arms around Mrs. Penfield and they

kissed. I tried not to stare at them; Lisle nudged me, smiling, and rolled her eyes. Then Mr. Penfield walked up to me wearing a suit that looked like he hadn't sat down in it all day. I had no idea what kind of work he did, but it didn't matter; he fit in perfectly anywhere. Except, of course, in my house.

"Well, hello, Eve," he said enthusiastically. "It's nice to meet you. Your family recently moved into the Whittaker house. Correct?"

I nodded. Of course Lisle knew which house was mine; my stupid attempt at confusing her was just . . . stupid.

"A little updating and that house will be as good as new," he said, rubbing his hands together vigorously. "It's always nice to have a new family in the neighborhood."

I smiled.

"Well, shall we all sit down?" asked Mrs. Penfield.

"Absolutely," answered Mr. Penfield eagerly. "I'm so hungry I could eat a horse!"

"You mean a *ham*, darling," piped Mrs. Penfield.

We all chuckled as we moved into the dining room.

"Eve," said Mrs. Penfield. "Why don't you sit there, next to Lisle?"

I sat down. The table top was dazzling with its tall crystal glasses and silver bowls; slivers of light shimmered from the glass chandelier. I gazed at my reflection in the cream-colored plate and hoped that good table manners weren't something you forgot if you didn't practice them. I pulled my chair in carefully, unfolded my cream-colored linen napkin, and put it in my lap.

Mrs. Penfield disappeared into the kitchen. On the table there was a basket of little white rolls in row formations. Lisle took one, put it on her plate, and passed the basket to me. I took one and passed to Mrs. Penfield, but she wasn't here so I put one on her plate. Lisle gave me a look so I picked it up and put it back. She gave me another look. I started to sweat.

"So, any hobbies? Musical instruments?" Mr. Penfield smiled at me expectantly. I swear his teeth twinkled in the light.

"Um, no. Well, I like to read," I said. "And write."
Silence.

"Read and write?" he asked, looking mildly confused.

"Yep. Read and write," I repeated, like a parrot.

"You do?" asked Lisle. "I hate writing. I think it's *sooo* boring."

"Our son, Chipper, is a writer for his prep school yearbook, *The Fighting Titan*. Maybe you've heard of it," remarked Mrs. Penfield as she backed into the dining room carrying a silver platter.

"Let me help you, darling," said Mr. Penfield, getting up to hold the door.

"Thank you, angel," said Mrs. Penfield.

I looked at Lisle to see how she was taking this, but she was calmly taking micro-bites out of her dinner roll. I guessed she was used to hearing words like "darling" and "angel" said without sarcasm.

123

"I see that Bessie outdid herself, as usual," said Mr. Penfield, putting the platter down on a side table. Bessie? That can't be Mrs. Penfield's first name.

"Yes, she is a wonder in the kitchen," murmured Mrs. Penfield, now carrying a casserole with her oven mitts. "But she had to leave early today."

"So we'll do the dishes tonight, right, girls?" said Mr. Penfield. "Plates, please."

We all passed him our plates. He put a slice of ham, a slice of pineapple, some green-bean-onion casserole, and some scalloped potatoes on each plate. Although ham isn't my favorite food it looked pretty good compared to my recent diet. I cut off a big piece and put it in my mouth. Then I noticed that no one had started eating yet. And they were all watching me.

Very loud silence.

"Lisle?" said Mr. Penfield. "Or perhaps Eve would like to lead us in thanks this evening."

All eyes on yours truly. "No, thanks. I meant no thanks I don't want to do any thanks." I was trying to chew, swallow, and talk casually all at the same time.

"I understood what you meant," said Mr. Penfield calmly. "Lisle?"

Lisle looked at me and rolled her eyes. Then she lowered her head and said in a soft voice, "Bless us Lord, and this food which we are about to eat, from thy bounty. Amen."

"Amen," said Mr. Penfield.

"Amen," said Mrs. Penfield. "And *bon appétit!*" She winked at me and gave me a just-between-you-

and-me kind of smile. I smiled back. My mom used to smile like that at me, but she hadn't in a long time, probably not since my dad lost his job. It made me feel good but sad, too.

But luckily, I felt better when I started to eat. Everything tasted wonderful. I couldn't remember the last time I'd eaten such delicious food. I watched Lisle's plate to pace myself. I didn't want to eat a lot less or a lot more than her. I didn't want to finish up way before her or way after her. When she took a drink of water, I took a drink of water. When she patted her lips with her lacy cloth napkin, I did the same.

"So, Eve, how do your parents like the neighborhood?" asked Mrs. Penfield.

I swallowed my piece of scalloped potato quickly. "Um, they like it," I answered. I didn't want to get off my food pacing with Lisle. "They, um, think it's nice."

Mrs. Penfield gave me a wide smile. "Well, we just love it here. In fact, we natives call Park Forest 'Our Happy Hills' because living in such a beautiful place just . . . makes you happy!"

Either that or lots of ProCalm, my mother's best-selling drug.

"And what kind of work does your father do?" asked Mr. Penfield. He flopped another slab of ham with pineapple on his plate. I'd known this question was coming this evening, so I was prepared. Taking a micro-sip of water, I patted my lips and cleared my throat.

"He's a building contractor," I answered. I had no idea what a building contractor did; I saw it listed on the side of one of the HomePro bags. I'd decided against carpenter or home-improvement guy and I certainly couldn't say househusband. Since none of those were true, I chose the most fancy sounding.

"Oh, really?" asked Mr. Penfield. "Does he have any local contracts?" He slathered butter on a dinner roll and took a hearty bite.

"I'm not really sure," I answered, looking at my plate. I'd planned this, too—this *awful* part, where I acted like a girl who didn't know what her dad did because it was too boring and complicated. This was the worst part of my lie, but it worked, like I knew it would.

Mr. Penfield chuckled and shook his head.

"Eve's mom works, too," said Lisle.

Both her parents looked at me. My stomach clenched. I'd forgotten that I'd told Lisle this; I had to remember what I said.

"Your mother works, too?" asked Mrs. Penfield, putting down her fork.

"And what does she do?" asked Mr. Penfield, putting down his fork, too.

"She's, um, um." Come on, Eve, come on. Now I remembered: the medical field. "A doctor. Yes. A doctor. A surgeon. A brain surgeon."

"Really!" exclaimed Mrs. Penfield, even more fascinated. "I had no idea that a doctor's family bought that house."

"A woman doctor, angel," corrected Mr. Penfield.

"I know, Roger. That's unusual, dear, that your mother is the doctor."

"I haven't heard of many women doctors who are brain surgeons," said Mr. Penfield, chewing thoughtfully. "Are you sure she's not a gynecologist?"

I shook my head and bit my tongue. But after all, I was the one who was trying for an Academy Award in the dumbness category.

"But didn't you say that she was out of town?" asked Lisle.

"She was. I mean, she is," I stammered. "She's called away to do surgery other places."

"Well," Mr. Penfield said, leaning back in his chair. "That's highly unusual." He looked pointedly at his wife and then back at me.

I started talking fast. "She's very well known. In the brain surgeon community, of course. She's called away a lot to consult. On brains. All over the world." I pursed my lips to shut them up.

"I know I'm old-fashioned," said Mrs. Penfield. "But I think I have the best job in the world—taking care of my home and family."

"But not all women feel that way, darling," pointed out Mr. Penfield. "Some have . . . other priorities."

They were all watching me now.

"But if your mother is out of town, then who cooks and cleans for you?" asked Mrs. Penfield. She thought for a moment. "Oh, of course. You must have outside help."

For a second I didn't know what she meant. Like, from God? Then I knew. Bessie. I nodded again. Alicia could certainly be called outside help.

"Occasionally," I replied. "When we need it."

"I can't imagine how you could survive without it. But does your father do some of the cooking and cleaning?" asked Mrs. Penfield in a concerned voice.

"Uh, uh, a little," I answered.

"And speaking of cleaning," piped up Mr. Penfield. "I think it's my night to do the dishes."

"Roger does the dishes on Bessie's night off," explained Mrs. Penfield. "And on Sunday mornings, he makes the world's most scrumptious eggs Benedict."

Was I hearing this correctly? Mr. Penfield, the father with a full-time job, the guy who thinks that my mother must be a gynecologist if she's a doctor, does the dishes? My dad doesn't do the dishes *any* night, and never did.

"Well," said Mr. Penfield heartily. "I know that taxes on a two-income family can be murder. If your folks ever need some sound financial advice, just tell them to give us a holler."

Mrs. Penfield laughed. "They can give *you* a holler, you mean, dearest. *My* financial expertise consists of balancing the household budget."

"I have a question," piped up Lisle. "Whose expertise is dessert?"

"Certainly not mine," said Mr. Penfield. "Because no one would want to eat it."

As we all laughed, I looked up to see Lisle looking at her parents and smiling. I realized that I'd never seen that expression on her face before: an utterly sincere, spontaneous smile. And it hit me that these three people truly cared about each other—regardless of how superficial they might appear to me.

I knew right then, more than anything else in the entire world, I wanted to be a part of this superficial family, where the food tasted good and the dinner table was pretty and the floors were clean and the mother looked happy and the father looked happy and everything . . . was normal.

CHAPTER TWENTY-THREE

The next night the Belkin clan was sharing their cozy dinnertime meal. The usual house problems (which had gotten worse, of course) hardly bothered me tonight because tomorrow . . . ta da! . . . my mother was coming home. I was so relieved that I didn't even scream after discovering penicillin growing in some cottage cheese.

Tonight we were having Hamburger Helper with actual hamburger in it because Alicia had run to the store and bought some after my father discovered that no hamburger came in the box. He wanted to take it back to SuperFoods and raise a stink, but she talked him out of it. As a side dish, we were having our fifth (and, please God, last) serving of fruit cocktail that I'd opened ages ago.

"See, Eve?" My dad speared a yellowish lima bean with his fork and motioned to the counter. "It was very economical to buy these size cans. Each can provided enough vegetables and fruit cocktail for five or six dinners."

Since I didn't have anything nice to say, I didn't say anything. I glanced at the clock; my mother was due home in about twenty-four hours. Twenty-four more hours of "protecting" Dad. I couldn't wait to be rid of my responsibility.

The so-called brother walked into the kitchen, marking one of his rare guest appearances at home. He had just come back from the gym and was drenched. He went over to the sink, peeled his shirt off, and stuck his head under the faucet.

"Have you heard of the latest invention? It's called a glass," I remarked, slipping an unidentifiable piece of fruit cocktail into my napkin.

David ignored me. Alicia got up and got him a glass; he managed to fill it up himself. Then she spooned out some Hamburger Helper on a plate and gave it to him. He leaned against the counter and started shoveling food in his mouth. I noticed a drip of sweat fall on the floor. This was too much.

"I can't believe this," I said. "You're dripping sweat on the kitchen floor while we're eating!" If my mother were here he wouldn't have been allowed to eat dinner without showering or at least putting on a dry shirt.

He didn't even look up at me. "So?"

I looked at my dad; he was spooning up a mushy canned pear and didn't seem to care. Alicia, who had sat down next to Dad, gave me a look like, I know it's yucky, but don't start a fight. She put another serving of food on my dad's plate.

"Thanks," he said. "David, why don't you sit down at the table with us?"

"Can't," he protested, his mouth full of food. "I'd stick to the chair." He looked around the kitchen. "Hey, where's the butter?"

Alicia jumped up, went to the refrigerator, and got out the butter for him.

"Alicia . . ." I began.

"Whoops!" exclaimed my dad, jumping up suddenly. "I almost forgot. The Ryders game. It's on right now!" He ran out of the kitchen and returned carrying the small television. Moving the dishes on the table around, he plugged the TV in about an inch from his plate. David picked up his food and stood behind Dad. Alicia carried a bowl of lima beans over to the sink so there would be more room on the table.

"Whew, good thinking, Dad," remarked David.

"Oh, my God!" shrieked my dad, spraying some noodles out of his mouth. He was pointing at the television. "Look at that! They're calling interference. I can't believe it!"

I threw my napkin down and stomped upstairs to my room. No one even noticed that I left, except Alicia, who was pretending to be interested in the game. Even though I knew it was only twenty-four more hours, I couldn't help it; I was completely and utterly disgusted with my brother and father. Rita opened the door to my room with her nose and climbed on the bed with me. I lay down and closed my eyes.

Rita barked and jolted me awake; I must have dozed off. There was noise downstairs. It sounded like someone had arrived. Was Mom home early? I opened the bedroom door and heard a strange voice.

And then my heart stopped.

It wasn't a strange voice. It was a familiar voice.

Leaning into the hallway, I listened intently. Oh no. Oh, God. It couldn't be. But it was.

Lisle.

I flew down the stairs barely even thinking about what I was doing. There she was, standing in the kitchen, a stunned look on her face. I felt like I was in a dream; everything seemed hyper-real yet not real at the same time. But I could see the scene exactly as Lisle did. Near the door where she was standing were three brown grocery bags, one overflowing with empty generic five-pound cans, the other two just full of garbage. Rita had knocked one over. A milk carton, egg shells, and coffee grinds were spilled all over the floor. On the wall and stove near her were huge splatters of tomato sauce from when my dad let something boil over and didn't wipe it off. To her left was a tower of greasy cardboard pizza boxes. Every inch of space on the counter was filled: bowls of leftover milk and cereal, gooey pots of macaroni and cheese, cold soup, a pan with scrambled eggs, plates of half-eaten sandwiches, a half-eaten Pop-Tart lying in a pool of coffee—and the pots and pans Alicia used for dinner. Then, of course, there was the dinner table. An image of the Penfields' beautiful, sparkling table flashed through my mind. Square little dinner rolls in a silver basket. White linen napkins. Mr. Penfield in his clean, white shirt. The quiet peace of their house. And here was my father, in a dirty sweatshirt and a baseball cap, his eyes glued to the tube, yelling at the ref with a mouth full of food.

Needless to say, they hadn't noticed Lisle.

Alicia had gotten up and was standing next to her.

"There's a friend of yours here to see you, Eve," Alicia said. "What's your name again?"

"Lisle," I croaked.

My brother looked up momentarily from his stupor. "Like 'weasel?'"

Lisle nodded slightly, her eyes wide in disbelief. I forced myself to walk over to her. My legs felt like rubber. By now she had taken in the whole scene; I could see that she was trying to make sense of it.

And then I saw it hit her—the reality behind my lies—and her face shifted from amazement to understanding to . . . disgust. I realized then that this was it: The End. The end of the life I had made up, the end of the family I had invented, the end of the . . . new me.

I hadn't budged from my spot.

"Eve," Lisle whispered. Now she was looking down at the floor.

I think I made a sound.

"I . . . thought we might . . ." She was backing up. My brother and father were cheering loudly, out of their seats. Alicia had started to wash the dishes. Rita was eating something off the floor.

"We might . . . ," she continued, "talk about the interview. I thought that . . . since it's . . . due soon . . ."

I looked at her and our eyes met and I knew that she'd deliberately planned this visit to arrive at my house unannounced. I looked at the clock—6:05.

Didn't her father always like to eat dinner exactly at six? She had concocted a story to try to catch me and my family at this particular time. Her suspicion that I—and my family—might not be up to snuff was just too strong. Lisle needed to make sure that everything of hers—her parents, her house, her life—was superior to mine, but not *too* superior. I was only supposed to be a few notches down, not an entire universe away.

Lisle could not meet my eye for more than a second; she looked away. I must have looked as awful as I felt. Making this sudden entrance into my home, Lisle got much more than she bargained for.

"So, I, um, guess this isn't, uh, such a good time," she stammered, her back against the door. "I'll, um, see you . . . tomorrow."

And she was gone. She was probably in our house for a total of two minutes. Alicia now had her Walkman on; she was singing softly as she loaded the dishwasher. My dad looked up from the television; the game was over.

"Was someone here?"

And that did it, I couldn't hold back any longer. Enraged, I wheeled around to face my father and screamed, "*DAD!* You've wrecked everything!"

"What?" He turned off the television and stood up. "What's wrong? What did I do?"

"You did NOTHING! That's what you did! NOTHING!"

I saw the bag with the empty five-pound cans and

kicked it hard. The bag toppled over and the cans clattered all over the floor. Alicia and David stared at me.

"Eve! Control yourself!" my dad shouted. "What are you talking about? I 'did nothing.' What do you mean?"

I was sobbing between words. "All—my—life—you—and—Mom—have—said—how—much—you'd—like—me—to—have—friends. And—I—finally—did—it! For you! *But you didn't do anything!* You were supposed to be a househusband. You were supposed to take care of the house. *But you didn't!* All you did was buy stuff for a stupid new deck and a stupid new bathroom and a stupid new basement and you haven't even started any of them!"

My dad looked at me, stunned.

"I tried to help you like Mom asked! I tried to be good so you wouldn't have to worry about me. I tried to be patient and understanding. Remember the 'new leaf?' *You* were supposed to turn over one, too."

My dad was holding up his hands now. "Okay, Eve, the kitchen is messy, dirty even. But is that worth getting so upset about? Will it really matter to your friend how your kitchen looks?"

I made a scornful sound. "Are you serious? How things look are *all* that matter to her—her and the other girls you and Mom have wanted me to be like my whole life!"

He looked bewildered. It infuriated me even more.

"Don't you see? Now Lisle knows! She knows everything! She'll tell everyone! What am I going to do? When I show my face tomorrow I'll be the laughingstock of the whole school—*because of you!*"

I could see pain on my father's face now as I ran from the room and up the stairs. I went into my bedroom and slammed the door. My throat was raw from yelling. I got in bed, curled up under my covers, and closed my eyes. A little later I heard my dad come upstairs. He knocked softly on my door, but I wouldn't answer it. After a while he went away. I got up and opened my dresser drawer. I took out my essays and put them next to me on my pillow. Then I fell asleep.

CHAPTER TWENTY-FOUR

It was 7:30 the next morning and I was in the girls' bathroom at school, trying to swallow an aspirin. I told the janitor that I'd left my books in school overnight and needed to get in to do my homework before homeroom.

I'd gotten up early and left before my dad woke up. I was planning to stay out of the house all day until my mom got home, which would be around dinnertime. I looked at my reflection in the mirror. My eyes were still puffy and red from crying so much; I hadn't cried that much in years. I felt exhausted. I sat down on the floor and pulled myself into a ball, hugging my knees. I wished the floor would open and swallow me up.

Since my whole life was in ruins, there wasn't much point in looking "nice," so I was wearing my grubbiest clothes: torn blue jeans, red Keds, and my dad's old checkered flannel shirt that was soft and warm. Twenty-four hours ago I would have confidently predicted that I'd never be caught dead in these clothes at school, and here I was. At least I was comfortable in my misery.

I wondered how fast the news would travel: Eve

Belkin's kitchen is a mess. Her brother is a mess. Her father is a mess. Normal girls all over the middle school can recite in unison, "EEUUWWW! THAT'S SOOOO GROSS!"

Now my stomach was in knots and I couldn't even go home sick if I wanted to because my dad would be there. All in all, it was a pathetic situation: My home was so lousy that I had to hide at school. At school I had to hide in the sixth graders' bathroom.

The bell rang for school to start. I considered going to see the school nurse and then decided against it. I couldn't feel any worse than I did right now, so I might as well face my public humiliation. I went to the sink and put icy water on my face. Wasn't that supposed to strengthen you? I wiped my face on my shirt. I didn't feel any better and now my shirt was wet.

Finally propelling myself out of the bathroom, I walked down the hall to homeroom. I sat there, leaning my head on my hand, not looking at anyone. When it was time to change for class, I walked right next to the wall, looking down at the floor. I could tell that kids were staring at me, but I kept my head down.

I managed to get through my first two classes without uttering a single syllable or looking at a single person. But then it was time for English. And Ms. Harley. And Lisle.

I took a deep breath and walked into the room. Lisle and Kristen were laughing at something. So Kristen was back in. Gee, what a surprise. She looked at me with a little smile and I had a powerful urge to yank her scrunchee out of her hair and tighten it around her neck, just long enough to hear her say, "Like, ouch." As soon as they saw me they stopped laughing and looked down at their notebooks. No words were spoken. I slid into my seat.

Then I noticed that some other kids in the class were looking at me curiously. I'd forgotten that I hadn't ever dressed in these kinds of clothes at this school.

Ian and Lydia walked past me and stopped. Ian stepped backward and spread his arms in surprise. "Wow. New threads." He said it in a nice way, but I didn't know what to do so I just shrugged my shoulders and looked away.

Ms. Harley clapped her hands. "How are you all today? I'm so happy to see you!"

Everyone ignored her as usual.

She launched into a spiel about different kinds of writing techniques and even though I tried really hard to concentrate on what she was saying, I couldn't. Kristen and Lisle were exchanging notes to each other in a giggling frenzy. Everyone seemed to be looking at our table, staring at me. My eyes hurt from staring down at my notebook for so long; my hand hurt from propping up my forehead. I glanced at the clock; only four minutes had passed. Oh, God.

I tried to listen to Ms. Harley but didn't want to look at her so I looked out the window. There was a group of kids outside playing kickball. I thought they were eighth graders, but I didn't recognize any of them. What an idiot I'd been, wasting all my time on Lisle, never getting to know anyone else. And now, what will kids think when they see me? Oh, there's the girl who was kicked out of Lisle's group because she was a phony. Now who's she trying to be friends with?

Tears started filling my eyes again; I took a deep breath. I wondered how hard it would be to transfer to another school. Maybe I could at least transfer to some different classes for English and math. I could make up *something* to tell the principal. But she'd probably want to call my parents and then I'd probably start lying all over again.

I was already worried about what I was going to say when my mother asks me about my "new friends."

What was I going to tell her?

Ms. Harley, who'd been walking around the room, stopped right in front of me. I tried to focus on what she was saying.

"When you wrote your poems we talked about instances when the normal rules of writing don't apply. When an author deliberately uses incorrect English to get his—or her—idea across. When is it okay to do that?"

Lydia raised her hand. "If someone wants to write about her emotions?"

"Good. How might a writer do that?"

"Maybe by not using a lot of punctuation or by making really long sentences or really short ones." Lydia was wearing a flannel shirt that looked like mine.

"Excellent, Lydia. Anyone else?"

Brady raised his hand. "If you're reading a person's thoughts, sometimes it's just one long paragraph."

"Good. In other words, the writer might intentionally not follow the right form because it would detract from the emotional intensity," said Ms. Harley. "Does anyone know what it's called when you read someone's thoughts in a book?"

"Um, stream of . . . something?" asked Donny.

"Consciousness. Good, Donny."

Something dropped on the floor in front of me, between Lisle and Kristen. It was a drawing of a huge can marked 'Mixed Vegetables.' They tried to control their laughter.

"Kristen? Lisle?" asked Ms. Harley. "Would you like to share your joke with the rest of the class?"

Several kids turned around to look at us. I closed my eyes. No, please, no.

"Like, sorry," said Kristen.

"Where were we?" asked Ms. Harley. "Oh, yes. Stream of consciousness. How about other styles?"

Seth raised his hand. "How about using slang? That can be incorrect, right?"

"Right, Seth. Very good. That's called writing 'colloquially.' It gives the reader a feeling of intimacy, as if the two of you know each other."

"Like those essays in the newspaper," said someone.

My stomach lurched.

"Who said that?" asked Ms. Harley.

"I did," said Ian. "Those essays—Mouth Off, I think they're called. Doesn't that writer write colloquially?"

My heart was pounding. Ms. Harley was smiling.

"That's exactly right, Ian! In fact, let's talk about those essays today. How many of you have read them?"

I was cringing in my seat.

About half the class raised their hands. I couldn't believe it.

"And what did you think about them?" asked Ms. Harley.

I took a deep breath and braced myself.

"They're fun to read."

"Yeah. They're funny."

"They're deep," said Vanessa.

"Bitchin'," whispered Donny.

I licked my lips. They tasted like sandpaper. I couldn't believe it. *My* essays. Funny. Deep. Bitchin'.

"How does it seem as if she's talking to you?" asked Ms. Harley.

"For one thing, the stuff she writes about. Like gossiping in the lunchroom," replied a girl I'd barely noticed before. "We all do *that*."

Seth piped up. "Yeah. And I really hate it when my parents wonder why I don't look like my neat cousin, Matthew. I could have written that essay myself."

Several kids nodded.

Ian raised his hand. "I like her essays, too, but there was one that I didn't agree with. The one about flipping the omelet and how girls are expected to know certain things like that? Well, boys are expected to know certain things, too, just like girls. *We're* supposed to know what to do if the car breaks down or have no problem killing a monster spider in the bathroom." He shuddered. "I *hate* spiders!"

Everyone laughed, including me. Ian was right; I'd never thought that boys might feel they have to act in certain ways, too.

I had been sitting and staring at my notebook this whole time, too afraid to look at anyone. But now I had to. I looked over at Ian and caught his eye. He smiled at me. I knew he didn't suspect that I was the writer; he was just smiling at me. I looked down and blinked and two tears landed on my notebook. Oh, great.

Ms. Harley began to talk again, but I didn't hear what she was saying. Then she started to walk slowly to the back of the room. When she passed by my desk, she put her hand on my shoulder and gave it a little squeeze.

By the end of class I was pretty much recovered. Nothing like going from the depths of despair to new heights of joy in a fifty-minute English class. When the bell rang I gathered up my stuff quickly. Picking up the drawing of the giant can, I crumpled it in my hand.

Ms. Harley called out, "Remember, your interviews are due next Monday!"

I turned to leave and almost crashed into Kristen.

"Um, Eve?" She looked nervous and uncomfortable. "Um, like, Lisle? She, um, can't do the interview anymore. Like, okay?"

I nodded at her. Lisle couldn't do her own dirty work, but it still had to get done. Kristen breathed a sigh of relief and ran down the hall to where Lisle was waiting for her. I felt a little bad for Kristen. She was still in the chains of Lisledom.

Lydia, Vanessa, and Ian were near me; we all started walking down the hall together. It occurred to me that I'd never even walked down the hall with anyone except Lisle and Kristen since I'd started school here. Lydia turned to me. "You know, that's one of the coolest shirts I've ever seen."

"Thanks," I replied, looking down at my shirt. Yeah. "It's my dad's."

"How's your interview going?" asked Ian.

The interview. Now what was I going to do?

Vanessa piped up. "Seth's actually talked Ms. Harley into letting him interview himself. His *yin* versus his *yang*, or some bull like that. So right now I'm solo." She looked at me. "Want to team up?"

"Sure," I answered.

We all walked to our lockers. Ian's was down from mine. As he was getting his coat out he turned to me and remarked, "You know, you seem different today, more relaxed or something. Maybe it's the clothes."

I shrugged my shoulders.

"Yeah. You seem more . . . normal."

I stuck my head in my locker and laughed for a long time.

CHAPTER TWENTY-FIVE

As I was walking home from school, Lisle's bus passed me. I could see her profile in the window, determined not to look my way, and I wanted to jump for joy. I felt weightless, as free as a bird. What had started out as the worst day of my life ended up being one of the best. Not, perhaps, *the* best because I didn't want to rule out the day that I win the Pulitzer prize, or the day that my essays are syndicated in every newspaper in the country (like "Dear Abby"), or the day every actress in Hollywood wants to play me in the story of my life (adapted from my best-selling autobiography, of course).

I kicked at a small stone in my path. No, I almost forgot: The best day of my life will be when I start my new job as a writer at *DUH!* I'll have my own office and a fancy computer and no matter what I write my coworkers will call it "wickedly funny." And not only will my name be on the door to my office, but it will also be on page three of the magazine that lists all the people who work there. Mine will be at the top: Eve Belkin, senior editor.

And then suddenly an image flashed through my brain: a dark wood door with the name "Peter

Belkin" in fancy gold letters across the top of it. I hadn't thought of that door in such a long time. When I'd go to my dad's office, the first thing I would always do was run down the long hall past Mrs. Butler's desk, skid around the corner, and dash down the short hall to that door. It was like a maze; but at the end of it was my dad, who was always hiding around the door waiting to jump out and grab me. Long before I learned how to read, I knew exactly what "Peter Belkin, Parts Distribution Manager" spelled. I thought my dad was the most important person in the world.

And then I had an image of my dad in the shirt I was wearing. One day I went to his office after school and his name wasn't on the door. I'd known he wasn't going to work there anymore, but I guess I hadn't really pictured it. Inside, he wasn't dressed in his usual suit; he was in a checkered flannel shirt and blue jeans. He looked sad, so I told him that he looked nice and that I liked his shirt. When we got home he told me that since I liked his shirt so much I could have it. He said he didn't want to wear it again and that it would look much nicer on me.

And then I started running. Fast. I needed to get home as soon as possible. I raced down the block and turned the corner. My backpack was bouncing on my back. I yanked it off and threw it down on someone's lawn; I'd get it later. Right now there was nothing more urgent than getting home. I pivoted sharply around the last corner and there was my house.

Panting heavily, I ran up the front steps. The door

was locked so I pounded hard on it. After a few seconds, I turned to run around the back. But then the door opened. I looked up at my dad. In one hand he held a bottle of Lysol, in the other hand he held the vacuum cleaner. I threw my arms around him and buried my face in his chest.

And for once I kept my big mouth shut.

Mouth Off: Just Don't Do It.

You're at school and wearing your new shoes, the black patent-leather Nike sneakers. You just had to have them immediately so you took the half size smaller than you normally wear. They'll stretch, said the salesperson. But it's the middle of social studies and your right foot is killing you. You go into the bathroom and find a gigantic bubbly water blister on the part of your heel where the shoe is rubbing. You almost pass out it is so gross.

You take your shoe in both hands and pull it violently apart. Then you make a fist and punch inside where the toes fit, to try to stretch it out. Then you put it back on. Or rather, you try to, except that you can't get it on, it hurts too much. And you can't wear just one shoe home because you're wearing tights and it's fifteen degrees outside. You call your house, but no one is there.

So you limp home and as you're walking up the driveway, your mom drives up. You hobble over to her and yell, "Where were you? My foot is killing me. I have a life-threatening water blister and I needed a ride home!" She looks at you like you're nuts and says, "Today was the first day of my new job. Did you forget?" And you shut up because the answer is, yes, you did forget. You forgot that she was starting work again today and where the work was and maybe even what the work was. In fact, you realize that you've hardly seen her in the past few days. And come to think of it you don't even know what day it is. Or what time it is. Or anything else.

All you know is your new black patent-leather Nike sneakers are crippling you.

And then a niggling little thought creeps through your brain, just to make it all worse. . . .

You didn't even like the stupid shoes in the first place. They cost four months' worth of allowance and they're dumb looking.

So why did you get them? Because all your friends have them. Why? Because they all want to look like each other. Why? Because they're afraid of looking different; they're afraid of looking like themselves. They probably don't even know what looking like themselves *means*. But I'll tell you what it means.

It means looking how you want to look and acting how you want to act without caring if it's how a "normal" girl is supposed to look or act, according to *other people*. *Other people* means "friends" who don't really care about you; they just want you to look like them. *Other people* means whoever makes up "dos and don'ts" at stupid fashion magazines. *Other people* means the one who tells you that what you're doing isn't "ladylike" or "feminine." *Other people* is anyone who encourages you to be somebody other than yourself.

And don't think that it's just dumb kids who act this way. It's parents, too. They might not think that they have to get patent-leather sneakers, but they might think that they can't do something because it's not something a "normal" wife or "normal" husband does. (Will they look "manly" enough? Will they have to grunt and groan so people will think they are strong? Will they still look skinny, sexy, and have big boobs?) They worry so much

150

about how it's going to *look*—and what others might think—that they forget how it's actually going to *be*.

So get your old red Keds out of the closet and put them on. Sit down and ask your mom how her first day of work went. And give your new Nikes to the Salvation Army. If they'll take them.

by Eve Belkin